"SHE KILLED AMY!"

I gasped at the stark words. Why was this woman denouncing me?

"Amy died from pills. The pregnancy and miscarriage were contributing factors. But we know the real reason Amy died."

I felt glued to the spot even though she was pointing at me, her expression malicious.

Denise came to my defense. "Are you crazy?" she asked. "You can't talk this way. Why, you're libeling Ruthie."

"I am not worried about libel. The facts are clear," she stated.

The woman swiveled her head toward me again. "No, I do not think you made a mistake," she told me, her voice thickened with emotion. "You deliberately switched those pills to kill my niece."

Other Rx Mysteries by
Renee B. Horowitz
from Avon Books

RX FOR MURDER

DEADLY R$_x$

A RUTHIE KANTOR MORRIS MYSTERY

RENEE B. HOROWITZ

AVON BOOKS ◆ NEW YORK

This is a work of fiction. Names, characters, places, and incidents either are the product of the author's imagination or are used fictitiously. Any resemblance to actual events, locales, organizations, or persons, living or dead, is entirely coincidental and beyond the intent of either the author or the publisher.

AVON BOOKS
A division of
The Hearst Corporation
1350 Avenue of the Americas
New York, New York 10019

Copyright © 1997 by Renee B. Horowitz
Published by arrangement with the author
Visit our website at **http://AvonBooks.com**
Library of Congress Catalog Card Number: 97-93012
ISBN: 0-380-78620-6

First Avon Books Printing: September 1997

AVON TRADEMARK REG. U.S. PAT. OFF. AND IN OTHER COUNTRIES, MARCA REGISTRADA, HECHO EN U.S.A.

Printed in the U.S.A.

WCD   10   9   8   7   6   5   4   3   2   1

To Lorraine, David, and Alexis Horowitz; Steve Horowitz; Myron "Mike" Braunstein; and Arthur, of course

DEADLY R_x

One

"**H**ave you noticed how many more prescriptions we've been filling lately?" Louise asked. Her question surprised me. Although she's only worked here since August, my new staff pharmacist rarely wants input from me.

"It's seasonal," I explained. "We'll be even busier as more and more winter visitors arrive."

"Don't get me wrong," she said. "I can handle it."

I looked at Louise Rettenberg, trying to gauge whether she was concerned about her ability to work in a busy store. She's a recent pharmacy school graduate, at least thirty years younger than I am, and until now I considered her to be self-assured and efficient.

Although I'm the pharmacy manager, Louise has never confided in me during the two months we've worked together. She seems to talk more to our young technician, Karen, but the only personal conversation I ever overheard centered on Karen's latest boyfriend.

Louise, Karen, and me—Ruth Kantor Morris. More than half of today's pharmacy graduates are women, but our all-female pharmacy is unusual enough to invite comments from customers and other pharmacists.

"I'll check with Karen. Maybe she can give us a few more hours," I said. "But don't forget she's a high school student."

She looked puzzled. "I know that."

"Her schoolwork has to come first."

"Oh!" She tugged on the neat dark braid that reached

just below the collar of her white lab jacket, a nervous gesture I'd seen before.

"Do the customer rushes bother you?" I asked bluntly.

"Ruthie, I told you I can handle it."

She sounded upset and I hurried to reassure her. "I wasn't doubting your professionalism. Since I'm the pharmacy manager, though, I need to know about potential problems."

Louise was right; we were busy. People seemed to arrive in Scottsdale hourly from the east and midwest. I had even noticed a few Canadian license plates in the parking lot. Although most Arizonans call these seasonal arrivals "snowbirds," I prefer the polite term, "winter visitors." After all, many of them are my customers here at the Food Go pharmacy.

Compared to the weather they're escaping from, our October days are warm. After surviving another Arizona summer, however, I feel chilly in the early mornings and evenings. That's why I arrived at the pharmacy a little while ago carrying my white cotton cardigan—too warm to wear now, but I'm on the night shift. I'll need the sweater when I leave work this evening. Meanwhile, I put on my professional jacket and started to help Louise clear the backlog of prescriptions. We had no time to talk.

Louise's shift ended about an hour later. Karen, our technician, was off today, so I'd be working alone until closing. I tried to move fast to keep up with the flow, but as quickly as I filled prescriptions, they kept coming in. At one point, at least four people were at the window. Others took the opportunity to shop while they waited, which was one advantage of a supermarket pharmacy.

"Is my prescription ready?" A thin, thirtyish woman with dark eyes that darted from side to side and never looked directly at me was next.

I took her name and looked through the "will call" stack. Nothing. The Rx's we were keeping "on hold" for a doctor's telephoned okay also yielded nothing. The only other place to look, the stack waiting for incoming inventory, was another miss. I rubbed my forehead, wondering what I'd overlooked and checked the computer.

"Nothing here for you," I told the customer.

"Has to be. Didn't my doctor call you?"

"No. I'm sorry." I looked at the screen. The computer showed that we filled a script for Toradol, the new non-narcotic pain reliever, for this patient on the tenth of October and refilled it on the twelfth. Today was the fourteenth of the month.

"Toradol, that's right," she said when I gave her the details. "That's the one I want."

"I'm sorry," I repeated. "You got it already."

"How can you tell?"

That was an odd question, but I showed her the original written prescription with the stickers that the computer generates when we fill each script. By this time, five or six other people had lined up behind her. I would never catch up.

"Somebody else got my medicine," she announced to the crowd. "I never did."

"Would you like me to call your doctor?"

"Never mind. I'll take care of it myself." She turned again to the people behind her. "I didn't even see the doctor until today."

"That's strange," I countered. "Right here, in the doctor's own handwriting, it says October tenth."

I saw some of the other customers trying not to laugh, but a waiting teenager seemed lost in her own thoughts, and the older woman with her looked grim. Before walking away, the woman threw one parting dart at me. "Well, I don't care what you say. You made a mistake."

This was a serious accusation, and I glanced quickly at my other customers to see their reactions. I intercepted a few sympathetic looks, and the next woman in line even reminded me that it takes all kinds. I smiled at her, but thought it would be unprofessional to agree.

Working as quickly as I safely could, I finally got to the last of the line of waiting customers and saw that no new ones had approached. Maybe I'd have some breathing space to do some paperwork tonight.

The last people in line were the teenager I'd noticed before and her dour companion. The younger woman handed me prescriptions for an antibiotic, a blood clotting agent, and a pain pill. I felt a surge of sympathy, knowing she'd probably just had a miscarriage.

Although the young woman wasn't alone, she was the kind of patient I worried about. She was wearing jeans and a pink T-shirt that advertised a popular amusement park. A typical teen at first glance, but her eyes were bloodshot with dark smudges below, and she seemed to be making an effort to hold herself together. She was thin enough to appear emaciated, and her face was pale. I looked at the first script again. Her name was Amy Brookman. She was sixteen.

"It'll take about ten minutes," I said.

"Okay."   *

"Can you make it faster?" the older woman demanded. Her voice was deep, but I couldn't tell whether it was an emotional huskiness or her natural tone. She was about sixty, with well-shaped features and short, white hair. I thought she looked too old to have a teenage daughter. Neatly dressed in a black and white herringbone suit and crisp white blouse, she seemed to have just stepped out of one of the office buildings across the street from Food Go. I wondered if Amy had been left to face the surgery alone while mother went to work. That was unfair, I reminded myself. Not everyone could afford to lose a day's salary.

Usually, I hate it when people try to rush me. They can't really think I take my time deliberately. Amy, however, looked as if she couldn't stand up much longer, so I buried my annoyance.

"I'll do my best," I answered mildly and moved over to the computer. While the labels for the three scripts were printing, I pulled the bottles from the shelves and counted out the dosages. She was getting the usual—ten Doxycycline, the antibiotic, to be taken one capsule twice a day. Then, her twenty Vicodin pain pills for the cramps. I used the generic here to save her money. And, finally, the twelve Methergine to control the bleeding.

Taking the labels from the printer, I checked each vial before labeling them. Amy and the older woman hadn't moved or spoken to each other. I reached across the pharmacy window and showed each vial, in turn, to Amy before bagging them. "The blue capsules, the Doxyclines, are the antibiotic. You have to take one capsule twice a day for five days. Be sure to take them all." I paused a moment and added in my most professional tone. "That's very important."

She wasn't meeting my eyes, and I wondered how much patient counseling was getting through. At least her mother seemed to be listening.

"The purple ones are to stop the bleeding," I continued. "Take one tablet four times a day for three days. Be sure to take them until they're all gone, too."

Now she looked at me. I could see the sudden realization that I knew what her medications were for.

"The last ones, the white tablets are for pain," I said, keeping my voice as detached as possible. "Take one every four hours if you need them. That will help with the cramps."

"Did you understand, dear?" The husky voice was solicitous, and I was glad to see the girl's mother was supportive. Sometimes when a teenager is involved, the mothers humiliate their daughters by berating them right in front of me and any other customers who might be listening. And when boyfriends or husbands accompany the young women, their attitudes range from tenderness to abusiveness.

"Yes, Auntie."

Well, I had guessed wrong. As they left the pharmacy area, I wondered momentarily where her mother was. I would never know the girl's story, but she seemed so fragile that my heart went out to her. Both telephones in the pharmacy began to ring just then, and I forgot all about Amy. By the time I took care of the call-ins, more customers were at the window. The next prescription I filled was for Clomid, a fertility pill, but I was too busy to reflect on life's ironies.

Two

My memory of Amy Brookman revived with an unexpected jolt two days later when I recognized her picture under the headline TEEN DIES FOLLOWING MISCARRIAGE. The local newspaper had been campaigning against teenage pregnancies, and I guessed they carried the story to bolster their stand. In any case, I stared at the photo. Amy looked even younger than she had in person. Perhaps it was an old picture. She wasn't smiling but had the same serious expression I remembered.

I read the article. Amy had hemorrhaged and gone into shock before she could be helped. There were few details. The reporter said that the girl's parents were separated, and Amy had been living in Scottsdale with an aunt, her mother's older sister. The story served as a departure point for statistics about the difficulties faced by young, unmarried mothers. No one in Amy's family could be reached for comment.

"Did you read this?" I asked Denise Seaford after ordering my lunch at the Food Go coffee shop. Denise was a waitress there, and we'd become friendly after my husband's death two years ago. During the summer, Denise and I had suffered through the ordeal of a murder investigation. I still felt guilty when I remembered that, for a while at least, I had thought she was the murderer.

Denise, who'd been smiling when she seated me, turned pale. "I wonder sometimes what would've happened if Craig and I had kids," she said.

"Did you want children?" I never had the nerve to ask before.

"Yes, but we were always saving for something or other. The time just got away from us, I guess."

I knew what was coming and braced myself. "What about you?" she asked.

"No luck."

"Didn't you see a doctor?"

"Of course I did! We both were tested and retested, but there weren't so many options then."

I thought about Bob and myself in the first years of our marriage. In those days, women expected to marry and have children. And I was no different even though I'd become a pharmacist at a time when few of us were in that profession. It took three miscarriages before I gave up.

Denise left to turn in my order, but I could see our conversation had to wait because two men had seated themselves at the opposite end of the coffee shop. I watched as she handed them menus, filled their water glasses, and took their beverage orders. They were in their forties, wearing white shirts and ties, but no jackets. I figured they were attorneys from one of the nearby office buildings. Engrossed in conversation, they paid little attention to Denise, but I noticed the way she looked at the one with thinning dark hair and old-fashioned horn-rimmed glasses and guessed she was interested in him.

Denise sometimes dated her customers, but I could never understand why these men faded from her life so quickly. She looked younger than her forty-five years, with a zest for life that showed in her flair for color combinations in her makeup and clothes. Today, she was wearing a lime-green blouse with splashes of old rose that would have looked unfashionable on anyone else. Her skirt matched the rose in the blouse and so did her makeup. With the dark green aprons supplied by Food Go for its coffee shop waitresses, the effect was surprisingly attractive.

Denise soon returned with the tuna salad and iced tea I always ordered. When the weather cooled off a little more, I would switch to coffee or hot tea. At this time of year,

I preferred hot beverages in the mornings and evenings, iced tea during the day.

"Do you know him?" I asked.

One of the things I like about Denise is her lack of pretension. Another woman might have asked what I meant.

"He comes in for lunch a couple of times a week. When he's alone, we get to talk, so I know he's divorced."

"Do you think he's interested in you?"

"I don't know. Maybe I started daydreaming about him because I get so lonely sometimes."

"Yes," I said. "No matter how busy we are, the nights are long."

"You have Michael now."

"I don't *have* Michael."

"Please don't think I'm envious, Ruthie. It's just harder for me now. I feel like I'm the only one who's alone."

I thought about Michael Loring. He had come back into my life with overwhelming impact when he had wanted access to some prescription files. Michael was sure the records would prove his daughter had nothing to do with her husband's sudden death.

"He just comes up from Tucson to see his daughter," I assured Denise.

"Could be, but he takes you to dinner whenever he gets to Scottsdale."

"We're old friends," I said.

Denise looked skeptical although I'd never told her that many years ago, Michael and I had planned to marry as soon as we both graduated from pharmacy school. "I don't know about that. You've been a widow for two years now. It's perfectly normal to date an attractive man."

"Men in their fifties aren't interested in their contemporaries," I said, knowing I sounded cynical, but unable to completely hide my uncertainties. "They prefer younger women."

The two men at the other table signaled for coffee refills, and Denise hurried across to their table. Then, she had to detour to seat a middle-aged, casually dressed couple, and took their order before coming back to me.

"I know you won't talk about your patients," Denise said, "but I can guess this Amy who just died was one of them. Otherwise, you wouldn't be so shook up."

"Am I upset?"

"Maybe you can fool other people, Ruthie, but not me."

The light above the counter was flashing, which meant an order was ready. Denise left to deliver it to the two men. Meanwhile, a group of high school kids came into the coffee shop, and I knew she would be too busy to talk for quite a while. I finished my lunch and went to the office to clock in.

My night shift shouldn't be too hectic this time, I thought. Louise wasn't scheduled to leave for a few more hours and our technician, Karen, would be in after school. I entered the pharmacy and, seeing at once how busy Louise was at the computer, waded into the fray.

"Have you been helped yet?"

Mrs. Wilmer, a white-haired woman in her seventies, handed me her prescription. She was a feisty one, despite the many ailments that frequently brought her into the pharmacy, and I always enjoyed helping her.

I saw immediately that the physician had checked off "Dispense as written," which meant I could not legally fill the script with a generic drug. I remembered, however, that we charged $43.55 for thirty capsules of the name brand, while the generic equivalent would cost her considerably less—under five dollars. I took the time to explain the price difference to her.

"Then, of course, I prefer the generic," she said.

"There's just one problem," I told her. "Your doctor always writes for the brand name. We've asked him to use generics before, but no luck."

"Let me try." The customer's tone was firm. "That is, if I may use your telephone."

I handed the phone to her through the window. "Yes, I'm sure *Doctor* is busy, but I want my prescription changed to the generic," I heard her say. A long pause followed. "Please go back again and tell him I can't afford the extra money. It's close to forty dollars more."

This time the wait was longer. "Fine," she said.

"Maybe *Doctor* would like to pay the difference."

After a moment, the customer handed the phone to me. I took down the change in the script and replaced the receiver. "I guess you got his attention.."

She laughed. "Would you believe it? He said he didn't know I felt so strongly about the cost."

A heavyset man in gray came up to the window as she walked away and placed his open wallet on the counter. I expected to see a card from some insurance plan. It was an ID from the Arizona State Board of Pharmacy.

"One moment," I said and unlocked the door for him. Periodically, someone from the State Board arrives unannounced to check on each pharmacy in the state. The examiner looks for outdated drugs, makes sure the pharmacy is clean, checks that the licenses of the registered pharmacists on duty are displayed, and audits Schedule II drugs—the ones the government considers most likely to be abused. These routine inspections are supposed to help pharmacists comply voluntarily with state and federal laws. As pharmacy manager or, as the state of Arizona puts it, "pharmacist-in-charge," I'm responsible for any violations the inspector may find, and I always feel slightly nervous until he fills out his report and hands it to me.

Karen, who had arrived just before the examiner, and Louise both stopped what they were doing and watched the man as though they expected him to perform magic tricks. I figured a State Board visit must be a new experience for both women. And although I'd been through so many of them during my years in pharmacy, I felt a sudden chill. My records were always in order; I couldn't understand why I was so much more apprehensive than usual.

After the examiner introduced himself as Jim Dalton, I waited for him to begin inspecting the pharmacy. Instead, he asked me to call up Amy Brookman's records on the computer.

Not a routine visit, I thought. For some reason, though, my nervousness increased as I busied myself printing out the information Dalton wanted.

"Her visit on the fourteenth was the first time here?"

I nodded. My throat felt too dry to speak.

Louise and Karen, still ignoring customers at the window, moved closer. "That's the young woman who died, isn't it?" Louise asked. "I didn't realize she was one of our patients. She must have come in after my shift ended."

Louise sounds like she's giving herself an alibi, I thought. What's going on here?

Dalton was looking at the printout. "Did you counsel her?" he asked.

"Of course I did." I knew I sounded defensive.

"Do you remember what you said?"

"I always say the same things to miscarriage patients."

He was silent, waiting for me to continue. I cleared my throat, willing my voice to sound natural. "As you see, she got the usual three scripts," I began.

"And you personally handed them to her."

"I was the only one here."

"How *busy* were you?" He emphasized the word "busy," and again I felt defensive.

"It doesn't matter how busy I am. I hand every vial to every customer separately, naming the drug, and mentioning the color as an added safeguard." My stomach was in knots. Why did I always feel guilty even when I knew I hadn't done anything wrong?

"Then I tell them the dosage, and I stress how important it is to follow the full regimen—to take the medications until they're gone."

He looked down at the printout. "And you filled the script for twelve Methergine to control the bleeding."

Now I understood why I was reacting so tensely to Dalton's visit. Before conscious thought, my body had known the danger I faced and had gone into fight or flight mode. I remembered the newspaper account. Amy Brookman had bled to death.

"How could she hemorrhage when she was taking Methergine?" I asked the question as it leaped into my mind.

"That's exactly what we're trying to determine," Dalton said. "We're analyzing the contents of the vial with the Methergine label. The tablets are purple all right. But

I have to tell you, to the admitting doctor at the hospital, they looked more like Coumadin.''

"Coumadin," I whispered. "No, that's impossible." Coumadin is an anticlotting agent, a blood thinner. It's probably saved innumerable lives of people who may be prone to heart attacks or strokes. But if Amy had taken a drug that prevented clotting after her miscarriage instead of one that aided it . . . No, it didn't bear thinking about.

"We were terribly busy that afternoon," Louise said. Now she sounded like she was trying to give *me* an alibi. I didn't want an alibi. There was no way I could have made such a mistake.

Dalton turned to her. "Didn't you say your shift had ended?"

"That's true. But when I left, we were way behind. I would have stayed and helped Ruthie clear the backlog, but I had an appointment."

What is she doing, I wondered. She's trying to protect herself, but now she's making it worse for me. Even though my physical distress was increasing by the minute, I had to say something.

"Mr. Dalton, it's not possible that I could have substituted Coumadin for the Methergine, if that's what you're implying. We don't shelve them anywhere near each other. And even though they're both purple, you know they don't look alike. Besides, no matter how busy we are, I always double check medications before I hand them to the patient."

"I'm sure you do," he said, but his tone didn't match his words.

Years ago, I'd attended an assertiveness seminar. It was time to make use of the techniques I'd been taught. I took a deep breath and spoke forcefully. "You'll find I'm very professional in everything I do. I think we should wait for the analysis before we continue this discussion."

He gathered up the printout, thanked me for my help, and left the pharmacy.

Karen looked like she was about to cry. I patted her shoulder lightly. "Don't worry," I said, not knowing whether I was talking to her or trying to reassure myself. "It will be okay."

Out of the corner of my eye, I saw Louise shrug. "Are you sure you didn't make a mistake?" she asked.

"Louise, don't even joke about something like that."

"I wasn't joking."

Three

I stared at Louise, unable to believe she had so little confidence in me. It's true we've only worked together for two months, but surely she could see by now that I'm methodical and careful. Because there were so few women pharmacists when I graduated from pharmacy school more than thirty years ago, I had known I must excel to prove myself. I had worked hard during those early years to be accepted as a capable professional. And the habits I developed then had never changed.

"Every pharmacist makes mistakes," Louise said in a low voice so the waiting customers couldn't hear her. "One of my professors told us that. What you have to do, he warned us, is minimize your legal liability. Cover yourself."

This was a new Louise. I was surprised at her cynicism and wondered what they were teaching in the pharmacy schools nowadays.

"Listen to me, Louise," I said as firmly as I could. "You know there's no way I could have made such a mistake. The Methergine is a coated tablet with white printing, not embossing like Coumadin. And Coumadin is flatter, uncoated, and a much lighter shade of purple."

"And if you just registered that the tablets were purple?"

"No. It's impossible. They don't look alike at all." I wanted to suggest that she transfer to another Food Go pharmacy if she had so little confidence in my abilities, but a customer was tapping on the counter. I didn't blame the young man. He'd waited patiently for at least ten minutes.

I walked over to the window and took his three prescriptions. "They're for my friend," he said, his expression daring me to comment. Doxycycline, Vicodin, and Methergine. His "friend" must be another miscarriage patient.

The scripts seemed to burn my fingers. I stood staring at them for a moment and, suddenly unable to cope, handed them to Louise to fill. At least the next customer, a middle-aged woman, would need some other medications.

I looked down and saw the same three prescriptions. This was becoming nightmarish. How could my head be burning this way when I felt so cold?

"It's for my daughter," the woman said. "I don't know what to do with her. Two miscarriages already, and she's only eighteen."

I'd heard this lament before and tried to look sympathetic. Any comment would be unprofessional. Karen was at the computer, doing the labels for the previous customer while Louise took down a prescription over the telephone. I would have to pull myself together and retrieve these medications from the shelves.

My fingers felt clammy as I took down the three bottles. I looked at their labels and compared them to the scripts. Then I checked again. When I counted out the Methergine, my hands shook, and I took four or five deep breaths to steady myself. The tablets were coated and darker than Coumadin. Methergine, without a doubt.

I gave the prescriptions to Karen to do the computer work. Louise was at the window, handing out the young man's medications. "And you must tell your friend to take these purple tablets four times a day for three days. Otherwise, she can bleed to death."

Good God, I thought. What kind of patient counseling is that?

Karen had the labels ready and I attached them to the scripts I'd just filled, checking each vial again. This time,

I also rechecked as I told the woman how her daughter should take each one.

"The instructions are on the labels, but be sure to go over them with her and be certain she understands," I said.

Louise was now behind me, looking over my shoulder. "Did you double check everything?" she asked.

The customer couldn't miss her words, and I felt my face flush from combined embarrassment, chagrin, and anger. "Louise," I said softly. "I've been a pharmacist since before you were born."

Now why did I say that, I wondered. I don't have to justify myself to her. What's happening to me?

Louise gave another expressive shrug and went to help the next customer. I wanted to talk about her scare tactics with the young man but couldn't bring myself to confront her. I walked into the back room. Ordinarily, I would ask Karen to unpack the order that was waiting. I started to do it instead, knowing I was hiding back there. I couldn't help myself.

Nothing like this had ever happened to me. I'd had encounters with addicts who presented forged prescriptions. Only two months ago, I escaped from a murderer who tried to drown me in my own swimming pool. But this was different.

In the quiet back room of the pharmacy, I thought about Amy Brookman. Could I have made a mistake? Not one like that, I told myself. I probed to see if my reaction was wishful thinking or self-delusion. If I'd done nothing wrong, why was I so upset?

Louise left about an hour later, and my own shift continued with no further problems until I finished at nine o'clock that night. The next day, my Saturday to work, was uneventful except for a call from Michael.

"I meant to dash up from Tucson sooner," he said. Michael's vitality showed even in his word choices. When we were in school together, I never heard him plan to do homework problems or write a paper. He was always going to tackle the assignment or race by the library. "I hope it's not too late to ask you out for Sunday brunch."

His voice turned the telephone wires into a lifeline. I

wondered if I could tell Michael about Amy Brookman and my self-doubts. When we had been in love, all those years ago, I wouldn't have hesitated. Even now, if we were alone . . . On the other hand, if his widowed daughter, Betsy Stokes, was going to join us, I knew I could say nothing. I would have to wait and decide tomorrow.

Saturday evening, after I arrived home from the pharmacy, I found myself regressing to my coed years, to the young woman who so joyously dressed for dates with Michael. I remembered one special evening, a Sunday night dance at our synagogue. My parents had argued with me for days.

"You can't take that one to a dance at the *shul*."

"His name is Michael."

"I know his name. Michael this and Michael that. It's a household word around here."

My family had moved to Tucson from New York before I was born, so I was that rarity—a native Arizonan. I lived at home—no dorms for Ruthie Kantor—and my mother was always in the kitchen when I returned from classes at the university. She usually helped Dad in his drugstore for a few hours during the late mornings and early afternoons. No matter how busy the store was, Mama was waiting with a snack for me. In some ways, she was the stereotype of the Jewish mother. Not the kind some people joked about or vilified in recent years. Instead, she was the "yiddische mama" of song, the one whose "jewels were her children." In this case, child, because I was the only one she had carried to term.

"Ruthie, you know we want only good things for you."

"Mama, I'm not marrying him. I just want to take him to the dance."

"What's wrong with Bernie Levine? What's wrong with Stanley Harris?" When my mother followed this track, she could continue indefinitely. I once counted seventeen names before she ran out of steam.

"I enjoy talking to Michael. We're in class together. With other boys, I never know what to say."

Although I was a university student, my mother insisted

I have milk and cookies every afternoon before I went to take her place at the drugstore. Milk for strong bones. Well, that medical insight turned out to be surprisingly accurate. I wondered if Mama was also right about Michael. Would we have been happy if we'd married or would it have ended in divorce the way his eventual marriage to Betsy's mother had ended?

"My yiddische mama, I need her more than ever now." The words of the song ran through my mind as I thought about Michael and how much I still cared for him. It was the first time since he'd come back into my life that I'd admitted those feelings, even to myself.

As I remembered that dance so many years ago, I was rummaging through my closet, trying to decide what to wear tomorrow. The weather forecast was calling for just over 100 degrees. Temperature in Arizona is relative, however. In spring, we make bets as to when the thermometer will first hit that 100-degree mark. And despite our air-conditioned environments, we suffer when the temperature begins to climb.

Now, in fall, it was different. "It's just perfect today," people tell each other. "Only one hundred and one degrees."

When Michael turned into my driveway Sunday morning, I was sitting in the dining room where I could see the street from my bay window. I had decided to wear a rust and white print dress with a matching short-sleeved jacket. Now that the winter visitors were returning to Scottsdale, the restaurant probably would have the air cranked to their needs. For residents, that could be too chilly.

I watched as Michael walked up the path to my front door, knowing I couldn't be seen from the street. In the sunlight, his hair looked more white than blond, but the vigor of his stride denied the years that had passed. Before the door chimes sounded, I had time enough to register that he was wearing tan slacks, an off-white shirt, and a tan and navy tie. He looked wonderful to me.

"Ruthie." His tone was warm, but he made no attempt to kiss me. In this age of casual acquaintances who never hesitate to peck each other's cheeks, I could only guess he was deliberately avoiding a gesture that I might misinterpret.

We had only seen each other twice since August, when his son-in-law's murderer had nearly drowned me. Both times, Michael had taken me to dinner. Brunch seemed more casual somehow—not what we would have called a real date when I was young.

He held open the door of his gray Lexus for me and waited while I seated myself and buckled my seat belt. Since I had ceiling fans throughout the house, I was no longer using my air conditioner at home, but cars could still heat up quickly. Even in the short time Michael's car was parked in my sunny driveway, the interior had become uncomfortably hot, and I was thankful when he turned the motor on and the air kicked in.

We were awkward with each other for a few minutes. I asked after his daughter and whether she would be joining us at brunch.

"Betsy wanted to sleep late. But she told me to be sure and whisk you back to her house."

I knew his daughter was having a difficult pregnancy. She must be in her fifth month, I calculated. Several times, Michael had driven up from Tucson to be with her when she'd sounded despondent over the telephone. He had called me those times, too, but hadn't wanted to leave Betsy alone. I knew he worried about her.

"She tries to sound cheerful," Michael told me. "But I understand how much she misses Harry."

Despite an initial negative reaction to Betsy, my feelings toward her were sympathetic now. At least her inheritance from Harry Stokes and her father's support would see her through, I thought, relieved for her sake. Many of the young women I saw in the pharmacy seemed to have far less going for them than Betsy. I shivered as I remembered Amy Brookman and determined to tell Michael about her. He was a pharmacist, too; he would understand.

Michael had made brunch reservations at one of the luxury resorts on Scottsdale Road. We were seated in a corner near the windows, and I wondered if he'd requested that quiet table. I decided to wait until we'd taken the edge off our appetites and then confide in him.

A waitress brought champagne and we sipped it slowly, in no rush to join the crowd at the buffet tables. Michael told me a few stories about the hospital pharmacy he managed, not naming the patients, of course. I had no idea what he did when he wasn't at work or whether he was seeing anyone in Tucson. As far as I could tell, he lived alone, but I wasn't even certain about that.

How did one find out? I was new to the jargon of the singles scene but supposed I could ask if he were involved in a relationship. What was the term nowadays? Significant other. I could just hear myself saying that!

Not wanting to talk shop yet, I toyed with my champagne glass. Today, talking shop meant telling Michael about Amy Brookman and, although we were alone, I was strangely reluctant to broach the subject. "Let's get some food," I said finally.

We walked over to the omelette bar and gave our orders to the chef. While we waited for him to make the omelettes with our choice of ingredients, Michael stood close beside me. "Your hair is longer than it was in August," he said. "Now you look just the way I remember you."

"I've been letting it grow since summer's over."

For a moment, I thought he was about to put his arm around me, but he suddenly moved away to take the plate the chef held out. "Mushrooms, cheese, and salsa," Michael said. "This must be yours."

His own omelette, which came up next, was topped with ham. As we reseated ourselves, he glanced at the meat and back at me. "This wasn't too sensitive on my part. Does the ham offend you?"

Michael had told me back in August, the first time we had dinner together, that he would have encouraged me to keep my traditions, even though our religions were different. "No," I said. "I think I told you Bob wasn't observant. We never had pork or shellfish in our own home—I couldn't bring myself to do that—but he ate it elsewhere."

"Do you realize, Ruthie, we never discussed how to

make it work? You and your parents were so insistent that you could never marry a non-Jew.''

I wondered why he was bringing that up now. It had been so many years ago, and we were very different people today. So different that two months ago, I'd even suspected Michael of murder. I looked down at my plate and ignored the question.

''For a while, I was rather bitter,'' Michael said. ''Please don't misunderstand; I'm not criticizing.''

He wasn't eating much, but I deliberately concentrated on my omelette to avoid replying. The salsa suddenly seemed too spicy to bear.

''Over the years, I gathered up every book I could find about Judaism, and I thought for a time I had some idea why you wouldn't marry me. I don't think I really understood then.''

''Let's not dwell on the past, Michael.''

''This is something I feel compelled to tell you,'' he continued. ''Have you been to the new holocaust museum?''

''Not yet.''

''I flew over to Washington, D.C. earlier this year for a hospital pharmacy convention. It was just before we met again.''

He concentrated on me with that vitality I remembered so well. The waitress came by to refill our champagne glasses, but now neither of us was eating or drinking. I had lost my appetite but, at the same time, wanted to cram food into my mouth so I wouldn't have to respond to Michael's words.

''I couldn't believe it when we met again. I'd been thinking about you for months.''

Now I was afraid he'd ask whether I'd ever thought about him. I didn't want to reveal my vulnerability. This was going to be worse than the first time. It would take me much longer to recover from Michael than when I was twenty years old.

''You've probably read how they create empathy at the museum. Each visitor takes on the identity of someone who was caught up in the holocaust. At the end, you discover what happened to your person.''

He paused and I was surprised to hear the catch in his voice. ''My person died at Buchenwald. I cried when I found out.''

No longer worrying about my own vulnerability, I reached out and put my hand on Michael's. I suddenly felt incredibly alive as he turned our hands so that mine was enveloped in his larger one.

''Yes, it makes you appreciate being alive,'' he said, as though he'd read my mind.

''And I wanted to tell you then, but I didn't know how to reach you.''

The moment was too intense. I was glad when the waitress came by and asked if we wanted clean plates. We returned to the buffet tables and filled our plates, seemingly absorbed in our own thoughts, but they must have been following parallel lines.

''How young we were,'' I started to say as we walked back to our own table. At almost the same moment, Michael said, ''We were too young to rush headlong into life.''

''My parents kept telling me we were too young. We should wait and see if we still felt the same way later on.''

Michael held out my chair for me. ''And did you still feel the same way?''

I hesitated for a moment, then decided to be honest. ''By that time, it was too late. You had already transferred from the U. of A.''

''But I hurried away from the University of Arizona because you told me it was hopeless, that we could never marry.''

''Michael,'' I said and repeated, ''let's not dwell on the past.'' I tried to erase from my voice traces of the despair I'd felt all those years ago. ''It doesn't do any good.''

We both had heaped our plates with the usual Sunday buffet food, but neither of us had tasted any of it. I picked up my knife and spread cream cheese on the two halves of a small onion bagel. Then I speared some Bermuda onion rings and a slice of tomato, added them, and topped it all off with smoked salmon. The smoked salmon looked delicious, a much better quality than I usually found in the Food Go deli. When I tried to eat, though, everything tasted like cardboard. I put the bagel down.

"I think we do need to talk about the past," Michael said. "If we're going to remain friends, and I'd like to, we have some cobwebs to brush away."

"Maybe you're right."

"For a long time, I was overwhelmed with resentment. I jumped past that years ago, but I need to understand some things." He had chosen a croissant instead of a bagel, and I watched as he broke it and slathered it with strawberry jam and butter—but he wasn't eating either.

"Go ahead, Michael. I guess it is time to take our memories out of storage and look them over once more before we throw them away."

"Since we met again last summer, I've thought about something you told me before we broke up. It was about intermarriage not being fair to children." He turned the full intensity of those blue eyes on me. "But you never had a child, Ruthie."

My eyes filled with tears, but I couldn't cry in front of him. I concentrated on rearranging the food on my plate until I could control myself. "It wasn't intentional."

"Another irony," he said. This time it was Michael who reached out for my hand. "Ruthie, I'm sorry. I didn't intend to hurt you, but I just had to know."

"The early years, when Bob and I wanted a child so badly—that was when it hurt. Women would come into the pharmacy with their new babies, and I'd wonder why not me. But it's a long time since I felt that way."

He was silent, but I could sense his doubts. I hurried to be absolutely truthful. "Lately, since Bob's death, I've thought about children again. About how wonderful it would be to have family now."

At Michael's expression, I hurried to add with a little laugh for emphasis, "Don't worry. These bouts of self-pity don't happen very often." In reality, I despised myself when self-pity took over, and I couldn't understand why I'd revealed so much to him. "It's just lately I seem to see so many miscarriage patients at my pharmacy. They remind me of my own experiences.''

''Isn't it unusual to get that many?''

''Yes. But we have one obstetrician in the area who specializes in difficult pregnancies. The way it affects me is strange, Michael. Some of his patients . . . some are just girls. I guess I identify with them, and it hurts to know the misery they must be feeling.''

''Did you and Bob consider adopting?''

I thought back to the early years of my marriage. Bob Morris was the son of a family friend. His name was one of the many Mama used to mention when she wanted me to go out with a nice Jewish boy instead of Michael. I didn't marry Bob on the rebound, though. When I finally agreed to meet him, it was more than two years after Michael had transferred to an eastern school.

I liked Bob right away. Although we were the same age, he had a serious air that made him seem older. We dated every Saturday night, as young people did in those days, and we might have drifted apart if Bob hadn't been drafted during the Vietnam War. It was while he served overseas that I realized how much I missed him. And when he returned, we decided to marry.

We lived in Tucson because I still worked for Dad. Immediately after I graduated from pharmacy college, Dad had enlarged the drugstore to make room for his only child. I enjoyed working with him, and I learned faster and smoother ways to make ointments, how to sell over-the-counter items, and other things that had never been taught in school.

The pharmacy was an old one, with paneled walls and thick shelves that still held many old-fashioned medicine bottles. We had no computers in those days, just an old manual typewriter, and if I made a typo in a label, I had to redo it completely.

Bob and I alternated Friday night dinners between my folks and his parents and, no matter which home we were at, we heard the same question each week, ''Well, when do we get a grandchild?''

After a few years, the pressure mounted. Our families

convinced us that I would carry to term if only I stayed at home and didn't work so hard—not an uncommon belief in those days. So I left my profession and bustled around the small house we had bought in Tucson, looking for things to occupy my time. And nothing happened. Meanwhile, one of the dreaded supermarket chains had opened across the street from Dad's drugstore. Their pharmacy drained customers from us, and when I wanted to return to work, there was no longer enough business to keep two registered pharmacists busy.

At about this time, Bob was invited to work at a startup company in Scottsdale. We decided the time was right to leave Tucson and, especially, to put 120 miles between ourselves and the parental nagging that, gentle though it was, never stopped.

I went back to work, this time at a pharmacy in a small medical building in Scottsdale and stayed with them until I transferred to Food Go sometime later. We bought the house I still live in and were a comfortable couple until Bob's death just over two years ago.

My retreat into the past had taken only moments, but I realized Michael was waiting for an answer to his question. "Yes," I told him. "We talked about it, and then we made the mistake of mentioning the possibility to our families." The ensuing uproar had been a major factor in our decision to move from Tucson.

Remembering how much parental approval or disapproval meant to us then seems unreal in today's world. Thinking back to the social climate in those days and trying to comprehend why it affected us so much is nearly as difficult as reading Jane Austen and understanding the way Emma catered to her father's wishes. Even after we moved, we were unable to ignore their opposition to adopting children.

I told Michael, and he wanted to know why they opposed adoption. "If they ever gave us reasons, I don't remember them." It was the truth. Either I'd repressed the memory, or they had felt reasons were unnecessary.

"And what happened after you moved up here?"

"I don't know. There were no more pregnancies. We

spent some time going to fertility specialists and found out the problem was with Bob.'' I smiled ruefully. ''Ironic, isn't it? I gave up pharmacy for more than a year because of an old wives' tale.''

''You haven't eaten anything,'' Michael said. ''I'm sorry I brought up such a painful topic.''

''It hasn't been painful for a long time now. I guess what happened last week is affecting me more than I realized.''

''Let's get some dessert and talk about it,'' he said.

We walked over to the dessert table and looked at the array of cakes and pastries. I chose a slice of pecan cheesecake and waited while Michael decided on a double chocolate layer cake. My appetite hadn't improved, but I tasted the cheesecake to avoid talking. You're foolish, I told myself. This is the opportunity you wanted. Michael's a pharmacist, too. See what he thinks about the Amy Brookman situation.

''Michael,'' I said hesitantly. ''Have you ever dispensed the wrong drug?''

He rose quickly and came to my side of the table. ''What pharmacist hasn't?'' he asked.

''If I really did this, it was a fatal error.''

I told him about Amy Brookman's prescriptions and about her death. Then I recounted the visit by the State Pharmacy Board inspector. Michael listened quietly, but he seemed to crackle with barely constrained energy.

''What I'm hearing,'' he said finally, ''is that there's some connection in your mind between your own miscarriages and childless marriage and the way you react to women who miscarry.''

''No, I don't think it has any bearing on this case.''

''Are you sure?'' Michael's words sent a chill through me that had nothing to do with the air-conditioned restaurant. ''Could it have disturbed you enough to substitute an anticlotting agent for the Methergine?''

That was when the doubts really took over. First Louise, and now Michael. I felt betrayed.

Four

Although Michael tried to apologize, we had very little to say to each other after that. And nothing more was mentioned about going on to his daughter's house. I tried to tell myself that Michael's questions were natural ones. There was no reason to take it so badly. Others would be asking me tougher questions; I could not be so sensitive about my professionalism.

Disappointment with Michael and expectation that the Pharmacy Board inspector would reappear at any time made for a miserable work week. Each day, I read every news item in the *Arizona Republic* and the *Scottsdale Progress Tribune*. I could find nothing about Amy Brookman, which heightened my nervous state.

By Thursday, I was too tense to carry on a normal conversation. To avoid Denise, I had lunch at home instead of the coffee shop and arrived at Food Go just before the start of my night shift. As I entered the supermarket and turned toward the pharmacy, one of the meat cutters stopped me. Jeremy Douglas is a big man with a soft voice that contradicts his girth and the shrewdness of his expression.

"Ruthie," he said. "Just the person I'm looking for."

I was accustomed to this opening from friends and acquaintances, usually on social occasions, and wondered what medical advice he wanted.

"Can we go to the lunchroom?"

The employee lounge, where many Food Go people prefer to have lunch instead of the coffee shop, was empty at this hour. Jeremy led the way to a table in the farthest corner of the long, narrow room and we sat down. He peered around as if expecting to find someone hiding under another of the tables. I decided he must need information about contraceptives or maybe something like Antabuse, which is a drug used to prevent alcoholics from drinking.

"How's my favorite pharmacist?" he asked. He always calls me that, and I remembered how he came to my defense back in August when Detective Moreway questioned me in this same employee lounge.

I managed a weak grin. "Fine," I told him, but the words seemed to stick in my throat.

"It's like that, is it?"

His comment didn't make sense to me. I hadn't been sleeping well and thought I must have missed some nuance.

"My little niece was buried today," he said suddenly.

What was he getting at? Did he want Prozac without a prescription?

"Hell, I'm not doing this right. Listen, Ruthie, you know they're not just empty words when I call you my favorite pharmacist. I don't forget how you telephoned just about every drugstore in Arizona to get Ritalin for my boy when there was a shortage." He leaned forward, and his voice was soft but sincere.

"I could see how busy you were, but you kept on until you found it. And then you had to convince that pharmacy I was legit, that my kid really is hyperactive."

"That's my job," I said, although I was pleased to be appreciated. Periodically, we experience shortages of Ritalin, which is the main treatment for hyperactivity in children, or attention deficit disorder, as it's called today. What happens is that the Drug Enforcement Agency establishes quotas for Ritalin manufacture. When demand exceeds supply, parents of children with this disorder find it very hard to cope.

"Sure. But not everyone cares about people the way you do. That's what I told all of them. I said 'Ruthie Morris wouldn't make such a terrible mistake. Something else must have happened to Amy.' ''

I froze. The cuddly bear had been replaced by a canny animal, whose acute gaze never left my face.

"Amy Brookman was your niece?"

"That's what I'm trying to say."

"But the aunt who was with her. She's not your wife."

"No, no. Not Lupe. I mean the mother's sister. Me, I'm from the father's side of the family. Amy's father and I are half-brothers. That's why my name's not Brookman." He got up suddenly. "You look like you need a cup of coffee. Sit here, and I'll bring some back for both of us."

Jeremy walked to the opposite side of the employee lounge where management had provided a microwave, small refrigerator, and forty-cup percolator. Coffee was available all day long, and employees paid a quarter a cup on the honor system.

I preferred iced tea but sipped the hot coffee without protest while I waited for him to continue his story. He wrapped his big hands around his cup but didn't drink.

"Ruthie, I didn't want to be the one to tell you. But I think you should know, so you can be prepared. Maybe hire a lawyer."

"A lawyer?"

"The family is going to sue you. I couldn't talk them out of it."

"No, it can't be." I could feel the rising hysteria, but I couldn't seem to modulate my voice.

"Don't you carry some kind of insurance? You know, like the doctors," he said. "What do they call it? Malpractice insurance, that's it."

Like most pharmacists in today's litigious society, I do carry malpractice insurance, just in case, but it would never cover the kind of award juries make nowadays. And that wasn't the point, anyhow. I pride myself on my professionalism and couldn't bear to be publicly accused of a fatal error. Despite the way my confidence plummeted when Louise and Michael doubted me and despite what Jeremy was telling me now about his family, I was sure I had not given Amy the wrong drug.

I thought about her, so young and so unhappy that day. What a terrible death and how frightened she must have been. If only I could relive the day she handed me her three prescriptions. No, I must stop wavering or they'd convince me that I caused her death.

Jeremy was still speaking, peering at his coffee cup and avoiding my eyes. "You probably know that Amy's doctor called the Pharmacy Board. And now the police may be looking into it."

"The police?"

"Didn't they question you?"

I shook my head, unable to speak. My world was crashing down around me, and there was no one I could turn to.

"The family doesn't want to wait for them to investigate. They got hold of a lawyer. Actually, he's a distant cousin of mine." Jeremy suddenly looked up at me and stood, slamming his coffee mug on the table. "You're not going to pass out on me?"

His bulky figure loomed over me, cutting off the light. Or maybe he was right, and the darkness was a physical reaction to his news.

I made an effort to pull myself together. "I'm okay. Tell me the rest of it."

"You know how people think nowadays. Anything happens and they want to sue everyone in sight." Jeremy returned to his seat. "They're going to sue you and also Food Go. I couldn't talk them out of it," he repeated.

I wanted to find out more from him, but the wall clock showed me I was nearly twenty minutes late. I had to get to the pharmacy. "Could we talk more about this?"

"Maybe I shouldn't have said anything. I didn't want to upset you."

"It's better for me to know," I told him.

"I guess we both gotta get to work now. But the wife said I should bring you to the house to discuss the situation. We want to help you."

Until now, we'd been lucky to avoid interruptions, but I saw Denise in the doorway with one of the young women from the bakery department. Denise came right over to our table.

"Your other pharmacist is complaining bitterly because you're late," she told me.

"I'm on my way," I said.

"Are you off this Saturday?" Jeremy asked. When I nodded, he said he'd be working until two o'clock. "Why don't you come here and I'll drive you?"

I saw Denise raise her eyebrows. "It's not what you think," I said as I left the employee lounge.

Like many workplaces, Food Go with its hundred or so employees was one huge gossip mill. I was sure I could trust Denise not to say anything, but the young woman from the bakery looked as if she couldn't wait to dish out this interesting tidbit. Well, I had more important things to worry about. And I faced one of them as soon as I reached the pharmacy.

Three customers were standing at the window, and Louise and Karen each had a phone to her ear. Karen smiled at me as I came through the door, but Louise grimaced.

Don't let it get to you, I told myself. After all, you're the manager here. A persistent inner voice reminded me it might not be for long.

I went to help the person who was first in line. He was a tired-looking man in his seventies who handed me a bottle with the original label on it. It was for 100 Pepcid, dated nearly two months earlier.

"This is my stomach medicine that I got a while back," he told me. His tone was mild, and I waited to see whether he had a complaint or merely wanted information. The bottle was empty, so I assumed he wanted a refill and started over to the computer to look him up. He called me back.

"I want to show you this," he said. He had a smaller prescription vial for thirty Pepcid, filled three days earlier. I looked inside and felt my stomach lurch. Two large, white pills—definitely not Pepcid—and the label had my initials on it.

It couldn't be a mistake. If I had made this error at a time when I was rechecking every prescription even more than normal procedure called for, then I could no longer trust myself. I stood there holding the vial, wondering what to do.

"Sir, did you have a question about this prescription?"

"Why did I only get thirty pills?"

"But where are they? I just see two here," I said, knowing I couldn't wait much longer to tell him about the error. To add to my distress, Louise had finished her telephone call and joined me at the window, about to help the next customer. She would hear every word.

The man smiled at me. I remembered him as one of the pleasant customers. At least, he probably wouldn't get nasty when I told him I had given him the wrong pills. That was beside the point, though. My professional integrity was at stake.

"These two pills don't mean anything," he said. "This here's my wife's medicine. I just needed somewhere to carry them."

The relief was so intense, I wanted to cry out. I quickly pulled myself together. "I don't understand, sir. What's the problem?"

He pointed to the original bottle. "I told you. Last time, I got a hundred." Then he lifted the smaller vial and repeated, "This time I only got thirty pills for the same seven dollars."

I walked over to the computer and looked at his record. His doctor had called in the prescription for thirty tablets with four refills, but his insurance company required a co-payment of seven dollars for each script. It didn't make any difference if the prescription was for thirty Pepcid or 100 Pepcid. Rather than argue, I redid his prescription, using the allowable refills, and checking twice to make sure they really were Pepcid.

Louise and Karen were chatting while I filled the next prescription. Although I was disappointed at Louise's reaction to the Amy Brookman catastrophe, I had always appreciated my new pharmacist's friendliness toward our young technician. The contrast with my previous staff pharmacist, who had considered himself too superior to treat technicians like human beings, still surprised me.

When Louise's shift ended shortly afterwards, I continued to work the window while Karen fielded telephone calls. After a while, business slowed down enough for me to come out from behind the pharmacy and straighten shelves in the health and beauty area. I don't often have time to "face" the shelves, but unlike some pharmacists, I enjoy the chance to do it. For one thing, I can keep track of these items for customer information. Often, the pharmacist is the only person they can find to ask when they can't locate vitamins or suntan lotion or whatever. Also, I can think while I "face," and I badly needed to think.

I started at the far end, knowing I could depend on Karen to call me if she needed me. The hair care displays were a mess and I moved along, pulling bottles and boxes forward in an even line, beginning at eye level with Food Go's own label shampoos. As I worked, I tried to solve my problem.

In reality, I had two areas of concern, but they overlapped. I feared I was losing my self-confidence, so much so that a few minutes ago, I'd been ready to believe I was making basic errors and couldn't trust myself to fill prescriptions correctly. I understood the cause. Not only had a patient of mine died because she took a blood thinner instead of a clotting agent, but I had also been accused of substituting that drug for the one her doctor prescribed.

And now, Jeremy Douglas had told me that Amy Brookman's family was planning a malpractice suit. Unless I could be sure that I'd filled Amy's prescriptions correctly, I could not cope. Yet, how was I to convince myself? Worse, without a firm belief that I hadn't contributed to her death, how could I convince anyone else?

I'd already tried to reconstruct that afternoon dozens of times. It was impossible to remember exactly what had happened. Suddenly, however, a calm feeling enveloped me for the first time since the Pharmacy Board inspector had come in. I reminded myself that checking my work was automatic, a habit so ingrained that there was no way I could have mistaken Coumadin, the blood thinner, for Methergine. No matter what anyone else believed—the inspector, Louise, Michael—I knew there had to be some other explanation for Amy Brookman's death. And when I met with Jeremy on Saturday, I would do my best to discover what really happened.

Five

On Saturday, I dressed as carefully as I had for brunch with Michael earlier in the week. This time, I concentrated on achieving a professional look. I knew that Jeremy Douglas and his wife believed in me. The two-piece gray dress, its short sleeves banded in white to match the white notched collar, was to bolster my own newly regained assurance. Just after two o'clock that afternoon, I followed Jeremy's white Ford pickup to his home. Jeremy and Guadalupe Douglas lived in an older section of the city, which in Scottsdale meant the house had probably been built in the early 1960s. The neighborhood boasted many grapefruit trees, and I could see the huge crates of the citrus pickers along the curbs. At the Douglas home, however, two large mulberry trees dominated each half of the lawn. We parked in the driveway and walked along a brick path to the front door.

It was a concrete block house, beige, with a brown shake roof and brown shutters. Only the paint colors distinguished it from the other houses on the street and, in fact, every third or fourth house was also beige and brown. Because these were older homes, I could see individual touches of ownership in the landscaping and add-ons like bay windows and brick planters.

Lupe opened the door as we approached it. Like her husband, she had a large frame, but she, too, was tall enough to carry her weight. If he resembled a teddy bear, she looked like the mother figures in R. C. Gorman's lithographs.

"Come in, Ruthie. Welcome."

Since her husband usually picked up any medications for the family, I had only talked to Guadalupe Douglas a few times at Food Go. I remembered when I first met her because Lupe had handled a potentially embarrassing incident with grace. She had come in with a prescription for her son's Ritalin. We have a number of Hispanic customers, and Food Go computers are programmed to translate into Spanish. So when I saw that the patient's name was Manuel and heard her speak to the little boy in Spanish, I asked if she wanted the label in that language.

Ritalin is usually prescribed to be taken "Tabs i qd," which means one tablet each day. To create a Spanish label, I could simply place the letter S in front of my entry. For Manuel's medicine, the label would read "*Tome una tableta cada día.*"

Lupe had laughed softly and said in barely accented English, "That won't be necessary."

"I guess I shouldn't jump to conclusions."

"Nothing wrong with that. It was thoughtful of you to ask."

I always enjoy the pleasant customers and, when I found out she was Jeremy's wife, I looked forward to seeing Lupe and Manuel at the pharmacy. Now, despite her warm greeting, I felt uneasy at what I might learn today from Jeremy.

He led me into a living room that mirrored the exterior beige and brown with walls of the former color and a brown and gold striped sofa. I sat in a comfortable armchair covered in a floral pattern of rust, gold, and taupe. The earth tones added to the relaxed atmosphere, and I marveled at finding one Scottsdale home that had escaped the "mauving" of America. Jeremy took the other armchair while Lupe sat on one of the sofas.

A marble cocktail table was laden with a platter of vegetables and chips arranged around a guacamole dip, and Lupe urged me to try some. I hesitated. This wasn't really a social visit, and besides I didn't want to crunch veggies while we talked.

"Let me fill a plate for you."

I agreed rather than be rude. We chatted about the weather until each of us balanced a gold cloth napkin and a plate of vegetables and chips, with a mound of guacamole in its center.

"You need to know about Amy's family first," Jeremy said. "On her father's side, Quentin and I are the only ones. But even though we're brothers, we don't see much of each other. I'll tell you about that later."

"If you're afraid to upset me, don't worry. I made peace with that one's bigotry long ago," Lupe said.

"Bigotry?" I asked.

"My folks didn't want me to marry Lupe. They considered her a foreigner even though her family's lived in Arizona more than a hundred years. Anyhow, Quentin sided with the folks. After they passed on, Quentin and I made up. Amy even used to babysit for us."

His features softened when he mentioned her name, and I thought he really cared for his niece. Lupe seemed on the verge of tears. I quickly looked away from the two of them and concentrated on dipping celery and chips into the guacamole on my plate.

"Quentin and Amy's mom split up, about two or three years ago I guess it was. Amy couldn't seem to settle down afterwards. She lived with her mother at first. You probably know what sometimes happens. Whenever they argued, Amy threatened to move out, to go to her dad. And she did, off and on. Then she'd argue with him and move back with Leila." He looked at Lupe. "Do you remember what they argued about?"

"The usual teenage tug-of-war, I think. But when the parents are divorced, it seems to be worse. The children can play one off against the other."

Jeremy had eaten some of the veggies on his plate while Lupe spoke; he cleared his throat before he continued. "Next thing you know, Amy wasn't getting along with her dad or her mom. So her aunt Virginia, her mom's sister, took her in." He looked at me. "She's the one you met."

"I didn't exactly meet her. She was with Amy that day."

Lupe nodded. "The day of the miscarriage."

Confidentiality obviously was not a problem here. Anyone who could read a newspaper knew about Amy's miscarriage.

"How did Amy die?" I asked. "Was the story in the paper accurate?"

They looked at each other. "We all knew," Lupe said. "About the baby, I mean. Quentin wanted us to talk her into marrying the baby's father."

"Was the father willing?"

"He's a high school kid. Like Amy was. Neither one was ready for marriage."

"He wasn't with her when she went to her doctor?" I made it a question, but I was pretty sure I knew the answer. If he'd been with her, I would have seen him at the pharmacy, too.

"No. Amy called Virginia from the doctor's office, and Virginia took off from work to help her," Lupe said. "It all happened so fast and so unexpectedly. She made a big fuss. Said her office was very busy this time of year. Wanted me to go instead. I would have, too, if I had a sitter for Manuel."

Lupe bit at a fingernail. "No, I guess that's not true. I wouldn't go with her because I was so upset with Amy's attitude about the pregnancy."

"We offered to adopt the baby," Jeremy said. "Manuel's a handful with that attention deficit or whatever they call it now. We used to call them hyperactive kids."

"I can't have more children," Lupe told me. "And Amy's child would've been a blood relation to Manuel."

I'm always amazed at the personal things people tell me. Maybe because they usually see me in my white jacket with the badge that says, RUTH KANTOR MORRIS, PHARMACY MANAGER.

"And she turned down your offer?"

"She was confused. She didn't know what she wanted," Jeremy said.

"I figure she would have agreed," Lupe added. "But I think her mother talked her into keeping the baby."

"They still saw each other?"

"Yeah," Jeremy said. "And never stopped arguing."

"What is Amy's mother like?" I needed as much information as I could get about this family that was going to sue me for malpractice.

"Frivolous. Just the opposite of her older sister."

"You probably noticed that Virginia's kind of like the maiden aunt you see in old movies."

"Frivolous in what way?" I responded to Lupe's comment first, but it was Jeremy who answered.

"She was only interested in going out to dances. Quentin met her at a dance, but then he settled down and she never did."

Lupe leaned forward and spoke in a near whisper even though we were the only people in the room. "She was running around on him. That's why Quentin wanted a divorce."

"Amy wasn't like her mother at all. She was a serious kid. Studious. And then after her folks split up, she changed."

"Oh, yes. Amy was perfect," Lupe said. "She . . ."

Jeremy didn't raise his voice, but his anguished tone stopped Lupe in mid-sentence.

"Lay off. She's passed on."

"Sorry." She seemed upset, too. Whether for Amy's sake or Jeremy's, I didn't know.

"She felt they'd let her down," Jeremy said. "It was like she'd do anything to get their attention."

"You think that's why she got pregnant?"

"I don't know." Jeremy shrugged his big shoulders. "I just don't know."

"But," I mused aloud, "surely if her purpose was to get attention, she would've wanted to keep the baby right from the beginning."

"Some young girls don't realize how much time a child

needs. But Amy babysat here. She had a more realistic outlook.''

"She had to cope with Manuel, and he's a handful sometimes." Jeremy sounded proud of his son's problem behavior, and I wondered if Lupe—who spent more time with the boy—would agree.

"This isn't helping Ruthie," Lupe said. "Let's tell her what the family is up to."

I listened carefully. My professional future could hang in the balance. It wasn't a question of losing my livelihood. Between our savings and Bob's pension and insurance, I could manage even if I stayed at home. My work, however, had been important to me all my life and since widowhood, it had taken on greater meaning.

Jeremy explained that the family had met at Quentin's place. "Even Amy's mother was there with her current boyfriend. Also, her Aunt Virginia and the two of us: Uncle Jeremy and Aunt Lupe. And we had invited the young man who was responsible for Amy's pregnancy.

"It was a free-for-all at first. Everyone blaming everyone else. But Leila, that's Amy's mom, got them to listen to her."

I pictured the scene as Jeremy continued his story. Leila had reminded them that pointing the finger wouldn't bring Amy back. "Nothing will bring her back," the young man had said. "Why wouldn't she marry me? I would have taken care of her and the baby."

"That's just what I mean," Leila told him. "We have to stop blaming ourselves. Amy would be alive today if they didn't give her the wrong drug."

"We can't be sure of that," Jeremy said.

Leila ignored her brother-in-law. "Luckily, we're talking about a big supermarket chain. We can sue the pants off them."

"That won't bring Amy back either," the young man insisted.

"No, but it will make them pay."

Virginia, who usually took the opposite view in any discussion between the sisters, agreed. "I was there with Amy. They were too rushed to give her proper attention."

"You told me the pharmacy manager was the one who filled the prescriptions," Jeremy said. "That's Ruthie Morris. She wouldn't make such a mistake."

"What's the good of having a lawyer in the family, if we can't call on him for help now," Quentin said, ignoring his brother's comment. "Let's get Eric on this right away and see what he can do."

"You mean that cousin of yours?" Leila asked. "I must say he helped you during the split. My lawyer didn't have a chance."

Quentin jumped up and started to shout at her. "You got more than you deserved. If I had my way . . ."

"Forget all that now," Jeremy told his brother. "I think we should talk to the pharmacist and find out what happened."

"Yes, it's too soon for lawyers," Lupe said.

Leila turned on her. "Easy for you to say. If it was Manuel lying there in his grave, you'd want a lawyer, too."

"You're wrong. I'd want to know what happened. But I wouldn't be trying to make money off my child's death."

"Quentin, that woman insulted me."

"Look, Leila, I'm not going to argue with my brother and his wife no more. We made up our quarrel, and it stays made up."

"Mr. Brookman," the young man said. He was a scrawny teenager who looked younger than his seventeen years. "We need to remember Amy."

He sounded like he was holding back tears, and Jeremy paid attention to him for the first time. "Of course we're considering her," Jeremy assured him. "That's why we're here, John."

"Tommy."

"That's what I meant. Tom."

The discussion continued aimlessly for a time. First Lupe, then Jeremy again, tried to get the family to wait before calling their lawyer. The family outvoted them, however, and Quentin was delegated to get in touch with their cousin Eric.

"And tell him we don't want him to drag things out the

way lawyers always do,'' Leila said. "We want him to find out exactly what happened. Take those depositions or whatever they do. And if we can sue Food Go and this Ruthie, let's get right on it.''

Lupe and Jeremy stood up to leave. Lupe was crying. "You're monstrous,'' she said. "Why do you want to hurt the woman just to line your own pockets?''

"She killed my daughter, and she's going to pay.''

As I listened to the end of Jeremy's account of this family meeting, I shuddered. It was even worse than I'd expected. If the girl's mother saw her death as a money-maker, there'd be no way to convince her that I had filled the prescriptions correctly.

"Did they call the lawyer? What did he say?'' The words emerged so indistinctly that Jeremy asked me to repeat them.

"Quentin's supposed to let me know.''

Right on cue, the doorbell chimed. Lupe went to respond and returned with someone who looked so much like Jeremy that they had to be closely related, although Quentin—for I assumed this must be Jeremy's half brother—was heavier than the meat cutter and clean-shaven.

I wanted to run, anything rather than meet Amy Brookman's father. This was a situation I'd never faced before but, I told myself, face it I must. And I knew I'd be up against much worse before I could prove I hadn't caused Amy's fatal hemorrhage.

"Eric thinks we've got a good case,'' Quentin said as soon as he entered the living room. Then he saw me and stopped.

"This is Ruthie Morris,'' Jeremy said and added with a defiant note to his voice, "my favorite pharmacist.''

"What is *she* doing here?''

"She's here because I invited her.''

"How can you have this woman in your house after what she did?'' His glance took in the food on the marble table and the half-emptied plates on our laps. "And you're treating her like any other guest.''

"I see that Leila won you over to her view," Jeremy said.

"You leave Leila out of this. I know damn well it's *your* wife who fixed the guacamole and all that other stuff."

"Are you trying to tell us what we can serve a guest in our own home?"

"I shouldn't have to tell you. You ought to know better than to invite her here after what she did to Amy."

"And I told you I don't believe she had anything to do with it."

"Then you explain to me how it happened." Quentin's voice rose as he turned in my direction. "Or maybe she can tell me."

I recoiled as I looked into eyes that seemed dark with hatred. "No, I don't know what happened."

"That's what I figured you'd say. You wouldn't admit you made a mistake."

"One thing I do know," I said. "I did *not* make a mistake."

"Maybe you can convince these two that you're innocent," Quentin told me. "But when our lawyer gets done with you, it will be a different story. Eric will make you wish you never saw Amy."

I shivered as Quentin raised his right arm and dramatically pointed his forefinger at me. I knew I must not start to doubt myself again, but I felt as though I were already on trial and wondered how I could ever clear myself.

Six

Although I was miserably unhappy, I couldn't get up and leave. An argument had broken out between Jeremy and his half-brother. They looked even more alike as they faced each other, lower lips thrust out and fleshy jowls quivering.

"You know Leila only cares about money. How many times did you complain to me about that over the years?"

"It's not the damn money."

"You know it is. She said so right there at your place the other night."

"Okay, maybe money drives Leila. But I'm looking for justice."

"It's not justice to do this to Ruthie," Lupe said. Until now, she had watched the brothers without saying a word.

Quentin suddenly sat on the sofa, all the anger rushing out of him like a balloon deflating. "Let's say you're right. Eric will get at the truth. He won't play games with us if there's no case."

"It wouldn't be the first time people've been sued because they had deep pockets," Jeremy said.

His brother appealed to me. "Don't you want to know what really happened? You should be the person who wants that more than anyone."

I didn't answer him but, for the first time, realized I couldn't sit by passively and wait for things to happen. If I was going to save myself, I must discover the cause of

Amy's death. The problem was that I had no idea how to go about it.

All the way home, I operated on automatic pilot and, for the rest of the day, I tried to plan. Only a few months ago, I had helped to catch a murderer when police suspicion fell on me and people I cared about, friends like Denise Seaford and Michael Loring. For an accidental death, I told myself, it should be easier to get information. I was sure Lupe and Jeremy would help.

Although the next day was my Sunday to work and I needed my sleep, I tossed restlessly that night, the same way I often did during the hottest part of the summer, the Arizona monsoon. It was a cool October night, though; the weather had nothing to do with my insomnia.

"You look terrible, Ruthie," Denise said when I made my way into the Food Go coffee shop for breakfast. I hadn't been able to cope with making it for myself.

I tried to brighten up. "That's a great way to greet a customer."

"I'm just not used to seeing you like this. You always dress so neatly and professionally and look at least ten years younger than your real age."

I glanced down at my pleated black and gold striped skirt. That at least was a polyester blend and looked fresh. My long-sleeved silk blouse, on the other hand, had crease marks from being stored in the closet during the hot weather, and I hadn't had the energy to press it this morning or to choose something else to wear.

"And that blouse always brings out gold highlights in your hair. But today it makes you look sickly," Denise continued. She handed me a menu without her usual flourish. "I'm worried about you."

"Thanks," I said, unable to keep a sarcastic note from my voice.

"If you pretend nothing's wrong, I can't help."

Denise had been there for me after Bob's death, and she had helped me to regain my equilibrium without encouraging self-pity. We found we enjoyed each other's company, something my other friends couldn't understand because she was "only a waitress." I no longer bothered to defend that friendship; in fact, I had gradually pulled away from those who judged people by their occupations.

I did need to talk to someone, to voice the fears that were keeping me awake nights. "Let's meet after work, and I'll tell you about it," I said.

Since the coffee shop opened hours before the pharmacy, Denise's shift would end earlier than mine, but we agreed to meet at 6:30 at a Thai restaurant, Malee's on Main, where we could sit and talk quietly over dinner.

On Sundays, I worked alone because the pharmacy was rarely busy when all the doctor's offices were closed. I caught up on some paperwork between prescriptions, transmitted a large order to our wholesalers, and was ready to leave only a few minutes after our 6 p.m. closing time.

When I arrived at Malee's, Denise was standing just inside the front door. She had put our names on the waiting list, which was a short one since Arizona's winter visitors were not yet here in full force, and we were shown to our table about ten minutes later.

We talked about innocuous subjects until our salads arrived. Denise had met someone new, through Food Go like most of the men she went out with. "Actually, he's a driver for our bread and roll suppliers. He's always been friendly, but last week when we were talking, I found out he just got divorced."

"They say that's either the best time or the worst time to start seeing someone."

Denise laughed lightly. She looked very attractive in her aqua and navy sunburst print, eye shadow that was one shade darker than the aqua, and costume jewelry that picked up both colors, interspersed with silver beads. "Could be. Well, I'll find out, won't I?"

She always went into these relationships so hopefully. Most of the time, the men seemed defined by her own romantic fantasies. The relationships never lasted long, and I still couldn't figure out the reason.

"Well, let's hear what's bothering you, Ruthie. Maybe I can help."

Denise was the most helpful person I knew. She bought

Girl Scout cookies from every Food Go employee whose daughter was trying to sell them; she was the first to stop by with a covered dish when someone was ill or flowers if they were hospitalized. What she did best, though, was to listen to our troubles. I knew Craig Seaford had divorced her to marry someone else, and I thought he must be a fool.

Since Amy Brookman's story had been in the newspapers and my information wouldn't breach patient confidentiality, I told Denise what I knew about Amy's death and the possible mixup of her medication. "At first, I blamed myself," I admitted. "But I'm sure I didn't give her the wrong prescription."

She took me through some of the main points again, especially the difference in appearance between Methergine and Coumadin. "I've watched you in action," she told me. "Not only when you're behind the pharmacy but in other things you do. You're always so exact, so careful. I know you couldn't have made a mistake like that."

"Denise," I said sincerely. "I do appreciate your confidence in me."

"Well, it's the truth."

"But I've gone over it so many times, and I can't figure out what else could have happened."

"If it wasn't an accident, Ruthie, then it had to be murder."

"Denise!"

"Well, I was right last time, wasn't I?"

She was referring to something that happened during the summer when her neighbor, who was also a customer of mine, had died suddenly. Denise was always so melodramatic about everything, a habit I usually laughed off as the result of too many late night movies on television. Suddenly, however, my sleeplessness and nervousness coalesced in a burst of irritation. This time she was dramatizing my professional life.

"Denise, please don't do this to me," I shouted.

An elderly couple at the next table glanced at us, then politely turned back to their own conversation. Denise's eyebrows contracted and she looked pained at my outburst.

"Ruthie, I'm sorry. Sometimes, I have an unfortunate way of saying the first thing that pops into my mind. It's spoiled a lot of relationships for me, but I don't want to lose your friendship."

"I shouldn't have shouted at you. I'm not myself."

"Let's forget that part. But we have to look at every angle."

I thought for a moment. Murder sounded farfetched, although I hadn't been able to come up with any reasonable explanation after the Pharmacy Board inspector talked to me. If I didn't dispense the wrong drug to Amy Brookman, how then did it get into the prescription vial I gave her? When normal means didn't seem to apply, maybe it was time to examine other possibilities.

"It never occurred to me."

"That doesn't mean it couldn't happen. Tell me, what is this other drug—whatever you called it—used for?"

"Coumadin. It's what's known as an anticoagulant. It thins the blood to prevent clots from forming. People take it who have heart conditions or have had heart attacks or strokes."

"A lot of people?"

"Quite a few," I said.

"And why would Amy die from taking Coumadin instead of the other medicine?"

"After a miscarriage, doctors prescribe a drug to stop the bleeding. Coumadin does exactly the opposite. I reviewed the literature after the State Board man told me what happened. Coumadin is a powerful medication; it's very effective. Like any other drug, however, it must be used carefully. And where there's any possibility of hemorrhage, Coumadin is contraindicated. Either it shouldn't be taken at all or it must be closely monitored."

"So you don't think the drug was prescribed for Amy."

"It's possible that she was taking it for some other purpose and didn't tell her doctor, but it's unlikely. She was much too young."

"Well, then, why are they trying to blame you, Ruthie?"

"Because that doesn't explain how Coumadin was

found in a prescription vial with the Food Go label and my initials on that label.''

Denise was silent. And although I usually loved the tasty peanut dressing on Malee's salads, my appetite was gone. I pushed some lettuce around on my plate until the waitress brought our entrées and I could let her remove the salad plate. Meanwhile, I thought about Denise's questions and my answers to them. Maybe it took someone who wasn't knowledgeable about pharmacy to make sense about what had happened to Amy Brookman. I was too close to the day-to-day practice of filling prescriptions to understand how other people would see it.

''There's only one other possibility,'' Denise said. ''Someone else who takes Coumadin deliberately substituted it for the drug Amy was supposed to get to control the bleeding.''

I felt as if my lungs would burst with the effort it took to keep from shouting at Denise again. Most of the time, the dramatic sense that underlined her vivid personality was charming; but now, when I seemed to be embroiled in a hopeless situation, her insistence that someone deliberately murdered Amy only added to my feelings of futility. I wanted to believe, but on the one hand, it was too easy a solution. And on the other hand, if it were true, how could I ever prove it?

''You don't have to tell me,'' Denise said. ''You think it's an off-the-wall solution, and you're trying not to be upset with me.''

I admitted that she was right and silently wondered why I had told Denise all my doubts and fears. It was pointless to lean on people. I had tried with Michael, and he hadn't trusted me enough.

''Why don't you start by finding out if any of the people close to Amy had access to Coumadin?'' Denise said. ''At least it will give you something to do instead of worrying about lawsuits.''

''It's not only the lawsuit that worries me. The State Board of Pharmacy could revoke my license.''

''That's all the more reason for you to find out what really happened.''

Again I thought over the possibilities Denise had raised. "There's one catch," I said.

"Probably more than one. But it gives us a starting point."

"I'm not sure it does after all," I said, choosing each word carefully. "Let's try to follow this through. Amy was young but certainly old enough to realize the pills looked different."

"Did she know what the first drug was supposed to look like?"

"The Methergine. Yes, I handed it to her, and I said . . ." I stopped, trying to visualize the scene. "At first, I didn't have Amy's full attention. But that changed as I told her about each medication."

"What did you say?"

"What I always tell them. After a miscarriage, patients get the same three prescriptions. I fill them and put the directions on the labels. Then, I explain how to use each one as I hand them over."

"But what do you say?" Denise repeated.

"I tell them the purpose and how to take the medications."

"Ruthie, this is like pulling teeth. It's so familiar to you that you do it automatically. Try to think of the exact words you used when you gave her that drug."

I closed my eyes and said in a hollow voice, not really believing it would make a difference, "The purple ones are to stop the bleeding. Take one tablet four times a day for three days. Be sure to take them until they're all gone."

Denise gasped audibly. "That's it!"

"Please," I started to say, not wanting more drama. And then I saw it, too. Amy knew only that she was supposed to take the purple ones four times a day. Aside from their color, she could have no idea what they were supposed to look like. For the first time, I acknowledged that Denise's scenario was possible.

Seven

"Let's assume you're right, Denise. Suppose someone deliberately switched Amy Brookman's medication and that's how she died." I tried to keep the despair from my voice. "I'm not a private investigator or on the police force. There's no way for me to question people."

"You've already started," Denise said, the excitement in her voice having the perverse effect of calming me. "You've talked to her father and her aunt and uncle."

"And what did I learn? Only that I'm going to be sued for malpractice."

"You learned quite a lot about the family dynamics."

"Nothing that points to a murderer."

"What about the boyfriend? Don't the police always look at boyfriends or spouses when a woman dies mysteriously?"

"I doubt whether the police see anything mysterious about it, Denise. They're more likely to assume negligence on my part."

"Think about it." She appealed to me as if I could do anything I put my mind to. And, for the first time, I started to examine the situation objectively. There were measures open to me instead of waiting passively for the other shoe to fall. For one thing, I could get a lawyer of my own, someone to cope with cousin Eric.

"I need a good lawyer," I said aloud.

"Have you ever been in the Cactus Plaza building

across the street from our Food Go? Lots of legal offices there."

"That would be convenient, but I can't go to just anyone. I need an attorney who knows what he's doing."

"Or what she's doing," Denise added. "Maybe a woman would understand you better."

"It doesn't make any difference to me," I said. "But male or female, I'd still better ask around and get one who's highly recommended."

Denise was quiet; I guessed she was thinking it over. After a moment, she asked whether I'd noticed the dark-haired man with horn-rimmed glasses who often had lunch in the coffee shop.

"His name's Sterling Harraday. He's with Davis and Harraday."

"But I don't know anything about him or even what type of cases he handles."

"He's very intelligent," Denise said and blushed.

I smiled for the first time in days. "Could do worse, I guess."

"Just talk to him. If he thinks you need some sort of specialist, I'm sure he'd recommend one."

I decided I would call Sterling Harraday the next morning. Maybe that would be better than asking around. Certainly, I should avoid telling too many people about Amy Brookman, and I was thankful that nothing more had appeared in the news.

This respite turned out to be short-lived. The next morning's local TV news featured Amy. A group campaigning against teenage pregnancies was using her death to organize a demonstration. A spokesperson for the group appeared on the program. She wore a well-cut turquoise dress with an antique-style lapel pin and either had a fresh permanent, or her light brown hair was naturally very curly. It was the sign she carried, however, that attracted my attention: NO MORE AMY BROOKMANS. In the background, other would-be demonstrators had unfurled a banner with the words, LET CHILDREN BE CHILDREN.

As I listened to the interview, I realized the group intended to exploit Amy's death to promote their own agenda. I wondered what her family thought about it and, in fact, I couldn't help thinking about Amy herself. This group was using her. Her death would frighten those who had no knowledge of the peculiar circumstances surrounding it, which was probably the intent of the demonstrators. Although I knew many people were concerned about teenage pregnancies, I felt it was unfair to exploit a dead girl.

As I listened, I could follow the path the group intended to take. Sixteen-year-old Amy had all the right qualifications to be their symbol. And bleeding to death, as the group's spokeswoman graphically described the hemorrhage, was a particularly horrible fate.

Denise had watched the same TV news and called me the minute the reporters went to another topic. "You can add Faith Sommers to our list of suspects," she said excitedly.

"Who?"

"You said you saw the news. I mean that woman. Didn't you notice the look in her eyes?"

"No, I was concentrating on what she had to say."

I could imagine a grimace on Denise's expressive face. "That news report just pinpointed someone with a serious motive for murdering Amy. The kind of person you should be looking for."

"That's rather farfetched."

"Make life easier for yourself, Ruthie. This couldn't be a better opportunity."

After another nearly sleepless night, I felt too tired to cope with this latest happening. "All I could think of was the publicity," I told Denise. "I was hoping there'd be nothing more about Amy in the media."

"But this is good news for you."

I couldn't agree. The only good news would be that Amy was alive, which was impossible. "I'll tell Sterling Harraday about it," I said. "He's going to see me during his lunch hour today."

"That's great!" She paused. "Look, Ruthie, don't tell him, but I think you and I should go to that demonstration Wednesday morning."

"And what do we do about our jobs?"

"First of all, this is more important. Anyhow, I already changed my shift so I can go there with you."

I thought how typical it was of Denise to act impulsively in support of a friend. "You're unbelievable," I blurted and then realized she might take my comment as a criticism. "I mean that as a compliment," I added.

Denise laughed. "Could be. I'll consider it one."

She was right about the demonstration. It was surely better than sitting at home and worrying. Besides, I would be working on the night shift and wouldn't even have to change my schedule.

After Denise's phone call, I felt surprisingly optimistic. This morning, although I put on an outfit I often wore to work, I pressed it carefully before I dressed for my appointment with the lawyer. I sat at my kitchen table and wrote out the main points concerning Amy Brookman so I could present them coherently and concisely to him. At 11:30, I got into my white Accord and slowly drove the three miles from my home to the Cactus Plaza Professional Building.

Although the temperature was only about eighty-four degrees, I automatically looked for a parking space under a tree. They were all occupied, so I unrolled my sunshade and placed it on the windshield. At least, I no longer needed to wrap a towel around the steering wheel the way most of us had to do during the Arizona summer.

The offices of Davis and Harraday were one flight up. I took the elevator and thought with a pang how different it would be if Michael were with me. He'd had no patience to wait for elevators when we were at the university. Then I wondered why I was thinking of Michael rather than Bob. If Bob were alive . . . No, I wasn't a helpless female who needed a man at my elbow. I was certainly capable enough to meet with the lawyer on my own and discuss the situation.

At Davis and Harraday, a middle-aged receptionist occupied a desk placed at right angles to the doorway. She was absorbed in the words on her computer screen but looked up and smiled when I appeared.

"You must be Mrs. Morris. Please have a seat and I'll buzz Mr. Harraday."

I sat in the kind of chair we used to call Danish Modern, gripping the teakwood arms as a spasm of nervousness suddenly went through me. You're doing the right thing, I told myself. Stop worrying.

Sterling Harraday came out to the reception area to usher me into his office. As I'd assumed, he was the slightly balding, dark-haired man I had noticed in the Food Go coffee shop, although I didn't remember ever seeing him at the pharmacy. I decided this wasn't the right time to mention the coffee shop.

His office was furnished in the same teakwood as the reception area with a huge desk in front of the picture window. Two armchairs flanked one side of the desk, and he motioned me to one of them. Instead of taking his own seat behind the desk, he walked around to the other armchair and turned it to face me, a posture that disconcerted me at first. I quickly realized that this gesture was designed to make our talk seem less formal and to put me at ease.

"When we spoke on the phone, I believe you mentioned you work at the Food Go supermarket across the street. Can you tell me what your job is?"

"I'm the pharmacy manager," I said. "In fact, that's the reason I'm here."

"Let me tell you up front that we don't handle labor-management disputes. I can recommend several firms that do."

"This isn't a labor-management situation," I said.

He apologized for jumping to conclusions, but his words had reassured me. I now knew that if he felt the case to be beyond his expertise, he would refer me to another attorney. "Tell me in your own words why you're here." His smile was warm, and I could see why Denise was attracted to him. "I'll try not to interrupt unless I have to clarify something."

I began the story of Amy Brookman, explaining how I filled prescriptions, what I remembered of the day of Amy's miscarriage, and what I had learned from the State Board inspector and from Jeremy Douglas. He took me

back over some of the details, especially my description
of Methergine and how it differed in appearance from Coumadin.

"And you are sure you filled the prescriptions properly."

"Yes, sir, I am," I said as firmly as I could.

"You realize it could mean someone changed the tablets
in that vial."

I was surprised he had reached that conclusion so
quickly. It had taken me days to arrive there and only at
Denise's insistence. "I've thought of that," I said, "but I
don't know how we could possibly prove it."

"We don't have to prove it. Only raise a doubt."

I gripped the arms of my chair. "But it would look very
bad for me."

"Cases involving medical professionals usually come
down to whether the person's acts would be considered
reasonable and prudent." He looked at me. I could see he
was waiting for my reaction.

"Yes, I've read that in the pharmacy magazines, but
I've also seen that pharmacists have been sued even when
they did nothing wrong."

"Anyone can sue anyone else. That doesn't mean the
case has merit."

The wood was biting into my hands and I made a conscious effort to relax them. When I remembered and told
him of cases I'd read about, however, I became more ag-
itated and my command of language broke down. "One
case. The pharmacist used a childproof cap. Someone voluntarily removed it. Afterwards. After he brought the medication home. A child ingested the drug and died. The
family sued." I looked across at the lawyer. "And a jury
awarded them millions of dollars."

"It happens," he said calmly. "But let's consider your
situation. I need to ask you some questions."

"I'm sorry," I said and wondered why I was apologiz-
ing.

"Did you get the full name of this cousin Eric they
mentioned?"

"No, but I can find out from Jeremy Douglas."

"That might be a good idea, but try to be casual about it. I don't think you want to let them know at this point that you've retained counsel." His face reflected a warmth that lessened some of the tension I felt. "That is, if you do want to retain me."

"I've never been in a situation like this before," I said. "I'm not sure what to do."

"Why don't you think about it? If nothing further happens, you won't need me. But if they do initiate a lawsuit, I'd be pleased to represent you."

He told me his hourly fee was $145 plus expenses. If we went to court, costs would increase, but he would try to keep this from going that far.

"There's one other thing," I said as he was showing me to the door. "We've only talked about a civil suit, and that's bad enough. But what if the police decide to prosecute me?"

"Do you have reason to believe they will?"

"I don't know."

"Is there something you haven't told me?" he asked. The genial expression was still there, but his voice had hardened. It seemed a hint of his courtroom manner.

We were still standing in the doorway, but he motioned me back to the armchair. I didn't know where to begin. No matter what I said, I'd sound like the legal profession's equivalent of a hypochondriac. Sterling Harraday waited patiently, although I realized he probably still hoped to salvage part of his lunch hour.

"A few months ago, the police questioned me about a murder," I began hesitantly.

"Another murder?" His tone was sharp.

Pull yourself together, Ruthie, I told myself. You can communicate better than this.

"That murder was solved," I said, "but not before I nearly became a victim." Keeping my tone light, I added, "I didn't mean to cause more conclusion jumping."

The warm smile returned and he leaned forward, encouraging me to continue. "Sometimes I think I was more frightened when the police suspected me than when the murderer came after me."

Sterling Harraday couldn't hide his astonishment. "But why?" he asked.

Maybe I should have looked for a woman attorney after all, I thought. A woman might understand how I'd felt when Detective Frank Moreway questioned me, suspicion in every word and gesture, making me feel guilty even when I knew I'd done nothing wrong. And this time, as far as I knew, I was the only one they suspected of supplying Amy with the wrong tablets. If Sterling Harraday says, "There, there," I decided, I would look for another lawyer.

He said nothing for a few minutes. Then it was my turn to be surprised. "I guess police routine is overwhelming when you aren't accustomed to it," he said. "As bewildering as it would be for me to face the array of drugs in your pharmacy." My expression must have given me away because he quickly added, "And that's meant sincerely, not condescendingly."

"I'll accept it that way," I said, "but you still haven't answered my original question—what if the police decide to prosecute me?"

"To your knowledge, had you ever seen Amy Brookman before that day?"

"No."

"I doubt whether the district attorney's office could consider any charge other than involuntary manslaughter and, as it stands now, there doesn't seem to be enough evidence for that charge."

As it stands now, I thought. He had hedged his words and, although I knew he'd intended to reassure me, I felt only despair at the phrase "involuntary manslaughter."

"That's a worst-case scenario," Sterling Harraday hastened to add. "I don't believe you will ever be indicted on that charge."

"Isn't there some way we can find out what really happened?" I could hear my own desperation.

He took time to think this over, too. "We could hire someone to investigate the backgrounds of the people involved," he said finally. "My professional opinion, however, is to wait. If we do anything at all now, we indicate that we expect legal action.''

I agreed that a conservative approach was best but left the offices of Davis and Harraday determined not to wait. Even an insect struggles to free itself when caught in a spider web. I would not do less to help myself.

Eight

On Wednesday morning, Denise called for me, and we drove in her old black Ford to the high school where the demonstration was to take place. Coronado High School is located near El Dorado Park in Scottsdale, surrounded by large parking areas, tennis courts, playgrounds, and athletic fields. The classrooms are in several one-story block buildings, painted schoolhouse red and trimmed in white.

Today, a chain cordoned the entrance to the parking lot just past a sign reading WELCOME TO CORONADO HIGH SCHOOL. FOR THE SAFETY OF OUR STUDENTS, ALL VISITORS MUST REPORT TO THE OFFICE. Dozens of people blocked the sidewalks, most of them waving signs toward two vans with the call letters of local TV stations that were pulled up on the street in front of the lot. We decided to park on a side street and walk back.

We circled the neighborhood and eventually found a parking space two blocks away. "I'm spoiled," Denise said. "I figured it would be crowded and warm, but I never thought about having to walk."

I looked down at her slingback shoes with their three-inch heels. She was wearing a sleeveless print dress in shades of green that I recognized as one of her favorites. With eye makeup that matched her bronze shoes and handbag, Denise looked as she always did, well coordinated. I guessed, though, that walking in those shoes and then standing around to watch the demonstration was going to be painful for her.

As we neared the high school on foot, we realized people were shouting, "No more Amy Brookmans," words that we hadn't heard through the car windows. I steeled myself. If I were to learn anything today, I had to mingle with people and try to talk to them.

I noticed a few women standing somewhat apart from the sign bearers, watching the television crews. They seemed to be onlookers rather than demonstrators, and we decided to join them first and then work our way along the sidewalk.

Denise approached a chunky-looking woman about her own age. "What's going on?" she asked innocently.

"It's a demonstration." The woman seemed eager to talk. "I saw the TV trucks. Figured maybe some celebrity was here. But it's really nothing much."

"How can you say that?" a younger onlooker asked. "Some pregnant teenager died, and they're trying to convince young girls to just say no."

"I thought that was for drugs." The first woman gestured toward another Coronado High School sign that said, DRUG FREE SCHOOL ZONE.

As she spoke, the shouting died down, and I realized we were close enough for the demonstrators to have overheard. A tall woman moved closer to us. She was wearing a nondescript rust-colored shirtdress, but I recognized the antique lapel pin I'd noticed in the TV close-up. Faith Sommers, their spokesperson, stood before me. She carried the sign that read NO MORE AMY BROOKMANS. With her other hand, she held onto a boy about four or five years old. If she had him late in life, Faith Sommers could be the child's mother, I thought. More likely, she was his grandmother.

She seemed rather young for that role, but perhaps Faith herself had been a teenaged mother, which could explain her reforming zeal. I wondered whether his mother knew the boy was out here.

A moment later, I realized he wasn't the only child in the crowd. It was hard to imagine anyone taking children or grandchildren along to a potentially explosive situation.

Well, the little boy would make it easier for me to begin a conversation with Faith Sommers.

Denise must have had the same idea. She bent to the child's level and smiled at him. "Hi, there, what's your name?" I had watched her charm children at Food Go and knew she genuinely liked them. The boy looked up at Faith Sommers as if he wanted her permission to answer. At her slight nod, he told us he was Bobby. This accomplished, Denise turned to the woman and ingenuously asked, "Didn't we see you on television?"

Faith Sommers inclined her head graciously. "I'm so glad my interview made you ladies aware of our crusade here." Her voice was soft and had a trace of a southern drawl.

Everyone wants to raise our consciousness these days, I thought. I looked closely at the woman, wondering if Denise could possibly be right in calling her a murder suspect. Faith's speech sounded cultured, she was well dressed, and she certainly wasn't the stereotypical fanatic I had expected to find. On the other hand, she had said "crusade," a word with loaded connotations for me. And despite her refined voice and appearance, she'd been shouting with the others only a short time ago.

To find out what I needed to know, I couldn't afford to be squeamish. "We wanted to learn more about your cause," I said shamelessly.

The other demonstrators had begun chanting slogans again, but Faith Sommers remained with us. "You heard about the little girl who died?" she asked.

For a moment, I was bewildered. "Little girl?"

She waved her placard at me. "Amy Brookman. She was only sixteen."

"Yes, I know," I murmured.

"Of course, you might call it retribution because she got into trouble," she said using an expression I hadn't heard in years. "But I forgive her. She really didn't know what she was doing."

I found it hard to meet her eyes when she spoke of Amy Brookman, but I glanced up in time to see her expression. It made me revise my opinion again. Faith Sommers glowed self-righteously. She was ready to "forgive" a teenager who had the misfortune to die after a miscarriage. And since I now wanted to believe Denise was right, that someone deliberately caused the hemorrhage, I had to control my anger at Faith Sommers's attitude.

"But how did the girl die?" Denise asked, sounding properly horrified.

Faith nodded toward the high school. "Don't you know the statistics? Every year in Arizona alone, twenty percent of all teenage girls get into trouble."

I had no way of knowing if her statistics were accurate. Swallowing nervously, I forced myself to say the words that were important to me. "Didn't I hear she took the wrong tablets . . . I mean pills . . ." I could sound just as naive as Denise. "They were supposed to clot the blood or something, but they made her hemorrhage instead."

"Where did you hear that?" Faith Sommers demanded harshly.

The little boy, Bobby, looked ready to cry. "Grandma, can we go home now?"

"Soon, honey. You go on over there and hold Miss Virginia's hand till I finish speaking with these ladies."

She pointed to one of the chanters and, for the first time, I recognized Amy's aunt among the demonstrators. Despite the warm October day, she wore a dark suit. She seemed thinner than I remembered, almost gaunt, but when she half-turned to reach down for Bobby's hand, I saw that her dark clothes were softened by a frilly white blouse.

Faith Sommers must have caught me staring at the woman, for she suddenly whispered, "I see you recognize Virginia. She wanted to bring the entire family to join us today, but Amy's parents were too distraught to come along."

I realized Denise didn't understand but before I could explain, Faith continued. "She blames herself, poor thing, for Amy's poor judgment. But I told her it's not her fault; it's the peer pressure." She stared at the high school again, her expression venomous.

"She's the aunt?" Denise asked. "Didn't I hear her niece was living with her?"

Good for you, I thought. I would never have had the courage to ask that question, but I knew we must extract as much information as we could get from every possible source. Watching Faith Sommers purse her lips, I expected her to turn from us. I could see her struggle between wanting to cut off our impertinent questions and wanting to gain converts to her cause.

"Yes, she took Amy in because the girl's parents weren't providing the right kind of home. Virginia set up strict rules, but she wasn't strong enough to change Amy's behavior. That's the saddest part."

Privately, I thought the saddest part was Amy's death, but I listened without argument. I could tell by the expression on her face that Faith Sommers was about to use this conversation for moral instruction. "Virginia was once like you ladies. She didn't give much thought to girls whose lives are in jeopardy, but now we have a staunch supporter. Now we have someone who stands here with us to keep these foolish young girls from getting into trouble."

I knew I was on rocky ground, but I had to get back to the most important point.

"Yes, I see what you mean," I said, "but if Amy died because she took the wrong medicine . . ." I let my voice trail off.

"That's a lie." Faith Sommers's tone had changed from the voice of the patient moral arbiter of a moment before. This was the second time mention of the real cause of Amy's hemorrhage had flustered her calm demeanor. I wondered what she really knew about the young woman's death. Maybe Denise was right about Faith's complicity.

"Are you reporters?" Faith Sommers suddenly asked.

"No, of course not."

"You certainly have peculiar questions. Well, I'm not here to gossip."

A few more people had joined the onlookers, and now I could see that one TV camera was panning the crowd. Faith noticed, too, and squared her shoulders and raised her placard so the camera could pick up its words. The other demonstrators also had observed the camera and went into a frenzy of slogan shouts.

This action didn't last long. Within moments, the camera was placed in the van, and the TV crew got in and drove away. The other van had already left. Now the demonstrators pulled their signs into their own vehicles and prepared to leave, too. Amy's aunt walked over to return Bobby to his grandmother. I waited, half expectantly and half fearfully to see whether she'd remember me. Even frequent Food Go customers usually don't know me outside of the pharmacy. Most of them never look beyond that white professional jacket with its name tag: RUTH KANTOR MORRIS, PHARMACY MANAGER.

Virginia didn't pay any attention to Denise or me. "You are ready for lunch, young man, aren't you?" she asked as she released the boy's hand to his grandmother. Her words had a rusty quality as though she wasn't used to talking to children.

"Can we go now, Grandma?"

"Soon, Bobby," Faith said. "Remember, I explained we have to help the girls who go to the big school over there."

I looked at Amy's aunt and willed her to recognize me, afraid of her reaction but knowing I couldn't clear myself without understanding more about these people who were using Amy's death to further their cause. She was about to leave; soon it would be too late.

Before I could say anything, Denise acted. "Ruthie," she said, her voice louder than its normal pitch. "You're going to be late getting back to the pharmacy."

Amy's aunt stared at me. "I thought I recognized you," she said. All of her features seemed to darken as she took a step forward and pointed her forefinger at me. "How do you have the nerve to show up here?"

"This is a public street," Denise said.

"I was not talking to you." Amy's aunt came closer to me. Her pale face was ashen as she looked down from the slight advantage her greater height gave her. I knew I had to control my fear and make her talk.

"What do you mean?" I asked, trying to keep my voice steady.

"Don't pretend with me."

"Who is she?" Faith Sommers asked. "I knew there was something fishy going on."

"This woman killed Amy."

I gasped at the stark words. Jeremy Douglas had warned me that Amy's mother was ready to accuse me because she saw a way to make some money, but why was the aunt denouncing me, too?

"She's a teacher in that school?"

"No, Faith. Not the high school. This woman is the druggist who gave Amy the wrong pills."

Faith Sommers looked surprised. "What does that have to do with anything? We're here to change the way these high school children behave."

"You do not understand," she said, her words stiffly formal. "Their permissive attitude started it, but this woman is the one who killed my niece."

Anyone could raise her eyebrows to appear surprised, but Faith Sommers really seemed stunned. Either she was a terrific actress or she had known nothing about the substitution of Coumadin tablets for Methergine.

"Amy died from pills? Not from the pregnancy?"

"The pregnancy and miscarriage were contributing factors. That is why I'm here with you today." Virginia spoke earnestly to Faith Sommers. "The family tried to keep it quiet because we intend to take legal action. But we know the real reason Amy died. The doctor gave her some prescriptions. One was supposed to stop the bleeding."

I felt glued to the spot even though she was pointing to me again, her expression malicious. This is what you wanted, I told myself. Let her talk; but my stomach was churning, and a headache was beginning behind my eyes.

"This woman is a druggist at Food Go. She gave Amy the medicines, but she gave her the wrong ones."

It was essential for me to stop this attack. I moistened my lips and forced myself to speak. "I check over every prescription very carefully. There is no way I could have made such a mistake."

"That is just what I told my sister," Virginia said.

"Then why are you attacking me this way?"

"You gave Amy a blood thinner instead of a drug that stops bleeding. And I agree that you could not have done it accidentally."

Denise came to my defense again. "Are you crazy?" she asked. "You can't talk this way. Why, you're libeling Ruthie."

"I am not worried about libel. The facts are clear. Even though Amy was bleeding so badly, I thought to take along all the pills so the emergency room doctor could look at them. He called in the hospital pharmacist, and they explained everything to me. They showed me what the pills were supposed to look like."

Ignoring Denise now, Virginia swiveled her head from Faith to me and back again. "No, I do not think you made a mistake," she told me, her voice thickened with emotion. "You deliberately switched those pills to kill my niece."

Nine

This couldn't be happening. It had to be a nightmare. I stood there, while Amy's aunt vehemently accused me, feeling like someone had taken me out to the desert and stranded me. I couldn't say a word. Soon, I realized Denise was talking again, but she sounded far away.

"What possible reason could Ruthie have to kill your niece?"

"We'll all find that out soon enough."

My mouth parched, my voice cracking, I made myself speak. The words seemed to be coming from someone else. "I didn't even know your niece. I only saw her that one time."

"We know all about you."

"Know what? What are you talking about?"

"I cannot say anything else now." She turned and walked swiftly away, leaving Faith Sommers, Denise, and me all staring after her.

"This requires an explanation," Faith said. "I can't have our cause damaged."

"*You* want an explanation!"

"I think I'm owed one."

"Grandma." Bobby tugged on Faith's hand. "I'm hungry. You promised."

"All right, dear. We're leaving now." She and Bobby started to walk toward a gray Buick Riviera. Faith unlocked the door. As she put Bobby into his car seat, she looked at me over her shoulder. "We have unfinished business," she told me. It sounded like a threat.

I had worried about Denise walking around in her three-inch heels, but I was the one who felt as if my legs couldn't carry me back to our parking spot. Denise gave me her arm, and I leaned on her as if I'd suddenly aged twenty years.

"She must be the one," Denise suddenly said.

"That's why we came out here in the first place. Because you thought it was Faith Sommers."

"Not Faith, the aunt. Why else would she accuse you?"

"But they're all accusing me. They'll do anything to get money from me." I knew my voice had risen, but I couldn't control it. "That's why I went to see the lawyer. Because Jeremy from the meat department said the family plans to sue me."

"That was for a supposed mistake. But this woman's talking about murder."

"So were you."

We had reached the car, and I sank back against the seat as soon as I opened the door and got in. I wasn't sure I'd ever get up again.

"It's early," Denise said. "I'm taking you back to my place for some food before we both have to go to work."

I was too drained to protest, too wrapped in my own thoughts even to be aware that we'd pulled into Denise's driveway until she cut the motor and removed her keys. She came around to the passenger side and opened the car door.

"Are you okay? Can you make it into my house?"

You can't fall apart, Ruthie, I told myself. With a day's work in the pharmacy ahead of you, this won't do. I made a determined effort to pull myself together.

My mind was so preoccupied with the accusations of Amy's aunt that I didn't notice the silver and gray Lexus pull into the driveway of the house next door. Denise's neighbor was Michael Loring's daughter, a young widow whose husband had been murdered a few months ago. Michael called to me as I started up the path to Denise's front door.

Although I was trying to walk without help, Denise was

supporting me as she had when we left the demonstration.
Michael must have realized that something was wrong. He
bounded across the two driveways, his energy contrasting
sharply with my own depleted stamina.

"Ruthie, are you all right?"

"Yes, yes. Of course I am." I tried to force conviction
into my tone.

"She's not all right at all," Denise told him.

"What's wrong?" Michael tried to hold my eyes with
his own, but I looked away. He turned to Denise and repeated his question.

"Some loony woman just accused Ruthie of deliberately—"

"Denise," I interrupted. "Let's not discuss it now."
Even if Michael had been more sympathetic when I told
him about Amy Brookman, I couldn't bear to stand in the
driveway discussing one of the worst moments in my life.

He directed that intense gaze toward me again. "I know
I don't deserve your confidence after our last meeting,
Ruthie. But I see that something is troubling you. Please
let me help."

"Thanks, but I'm really okay now."

"Why don't you come inside?" Denise asked Michael,
gesturing toward her house. "I think we need another
opinion. Especially since I heard you're also a pharmacist."

I frowned at Denise to show that I was against the idea.
Although I knew she was adept at reading people's expressions, she refused to acknowledge my body language.

Michael glanced back toward his own car, and now I
noticed he hadn't been alone. At first, I thought the woman
who emerged from the passenger side of the Lexus was
his daughter, Betsy Stokes. During the summer, when Michael and I met again after so many years apart, he had
seemed so solicitous of Betsy and so much a part of her
life, that I'd assumed a romantic interest until I had learned
they were father and daughter.

Betsy's blond hair was styled differently, I realized,
fuller with crimped curls. When this woman got out of the
car and crossed over toward us, I saw that her hair was

short and nearly straight, ending in a soft curl just below her ears. Unlike Betsy, who was expecting her first child, this woman was svelte. And she was closer to my age than to Betsy's.

The distance between the two driveways wasn't that great. In any case, she would have reached us quickly because she strode along with a brisk, no-nonsense step. Betsy, who seemed to have an unlimited wardrobe of expensive-looking casual fashions, would now be wearing maternity clothes. Michael's passenger also was dressed casually, but looked chic and attractive in well-fitted beige slacks and a cream-colored, long-sleeved blouse.

I waited for an introduction, but Michael said nothing. We stood there awkwardly for a few moments until Denise introduced herself.

"I'm Patricia Donleavy," the woman responded and shook Denise's hand formally.

"Ruth Morris," I said when she turned toward me.

"Ah, yes, Ruthie."

For a moment, I thought she must be one of my customers at the pharmacy. Perhaps she was another of Betsy's neighbors, and Michael had given her a lift. Then she touched Michael's arm to get his attention.

"Why are we all standing out here?" she asked. "Let's invite everyone next door."

I didn't want to jump to conclusions again, but this woman was obviously more than an acquaintance. Well, what did you expect, I asked myself. Michael is still an attractive, vital man.

Denise renewed her own invitation, and we all followed her indoors. Although she lived next to the Stokes's house, Denise's home was more modest. The Stokes's house had been built by the original owner of all the land in the cul-de-sac and had been extensively remodeled since that time. I'd heard that the latest renovation, completed just before Harry Stokes's death, had cost quite a bit. Harry had been wealthy, however, unlike Denise who struggled to make the mortgage payments since her divorce.

I saw the look of surprise on Patricia Donleavy's face as we walked through a small tiled entry hall into the living room. Seeing it through another woman's eyes this time, I noticed that Denise's favorite throw pillows with the sandpainting motifs couldn't quite cover her sofa's shabbiness.

Michael and Patricia sat on opposite ends of the sofa, but he put his arm across its carved wooden back as though reaching out to her. I took one of the armless chairs that made up the group, while Denise excused herself and disappeared in the direction of her kitchen.

I could think of nothing to say to Michael or his companion. Patricia spoke first. "Betsy's architect did such a superb remodeling job for her. Perhaps she would recommend him to her neighbor."

At least, this was a neutral topic. "Remodeling is rather expensive," I said, astonished to hear the curtness in my voice.

Michael seemed surprised, too. "Ruthie," he said again. "Please tell me what's wrong."

"Nothing," I insisted, "but I did mean to ask you how Betsy is feeling." He must have interpreted my quick glance at Patricia, for he went along with the change of subject.

"Much better now that she's well into the second trimester," he said.

"I don't think she looks like herself at all," Patricia contradicted.

Here was interesting news. It told me this wasn't Patricia's first visit to Betsy Stokes. To make conversation without resorting to weather reports, I was about to ask Patricia if she lived in Tucson, but I was saved from trivialities when Denise reappeared with a tray of refreshments. We helped ourselves to mugs of coffee and chocolate chip cookies.

"Do you both have the day off?" Michael asked.

"Night shift," Denise said.

Michael replaced his coffee mug and stood up. "Then we'd better run along."

"No, no. We have time," Denise assured him. I could have kicked her, but I sat there quietly, hoping she wouldn't reveal my problems in front of a stranger. It was too much to expect. Denise, who thrived on drama, couldn't be discreet when she had new listeners. I was unable to think of any way to silence her.

"We went to watch a demonstration at the high school," she said and quickly filled them in. "And that woman dared to accuse Ruthie of deliberately murdering her niece," she finished with a flourish, waiting for their reactions.

I saw that Denise could talk about the accusation because she didn't take it seriously, but I knew it could ruin me nonetheless. Bad enough for Michael to know what happened, I thought, but for this woman to hear it . . . this attractive blonde whose eyes were not on Denise while she spoke but moved from Michael to me and back again.

Patricia Donleavy surprised me. "How utterly abominable!" she said in ringing tones. "Some of these people are quite mad."

Denise agreed warmly, but Michael and I remained silent. "I remember years ago," Patricia continued, "when I miscarried. Before Roe vs. Wade allowed doctors to legally do a D and C on a pregnant woman."

Her words were clipped, and a look of pain crossed her face as she relived the experience. I saw Michael's sympathy reflected in his eyes and realized that this woman was important to him.

Patricia spoke again after a moment's pause that seemed necessary to gain control. "I knew something was wrong with the pregnancy, so I visited my gynecologist. He told me the fetus was dead, but he couldn't do anything about it. I must wait for nature to take its course.

"So, I went home and waited. And that night I hemorrhaged—not fatal in my case, but nonetheless a rather traumatic experience," she finished coolly.

Michael had reached for Patricia's hand while she told us the story, and I noticed how unhappy he seemed. She let him hold her hand for a few seconds after she stopped speaking. Then she removed it with a natural gesture, as poised as everything else about her.

"I wasn't angling for sympathy," she said. "I just get so furious with people who lack empathy." She turned back to me. "But now, what can we do to help you?" she asked.

Her concern for others was evident, and I could understand her attraction for Michael. I warmed toward Patricia despite my disappointment in seeing him with this lovely blonde.

"That's just it," I said. My voice sounded somewhat hoarse to me. "I don't know what can be done." And I've never felt so helpless in my life, I added silently.

She turned to Michael. "You're a pharmacist, too. Surely you can help."

"Of course, I want to help. But how?"

"You can find out if any of the people connected with Amy Brookman take that blood thinner—Coumadin," Denise blurted suddenly. "Someone close to her had to make the substitution. That's what I told Ruthie days ago, and I still think it's the only possibility."

Michael seemed startled by the outburst, and I knew he would never agree to Denise's suggestion. He already had voiced his doubts about me during that Sunday brunch, and I saw no reason to expect a change of mind. I had lost all chance of receiving the kind of understanding he had just shown to Patricia.

Well, it was my own fault. We had been apart too long, and our breakup had destroyed whatever feeling he'd once had for me. I was a fool to think we could be close again, even as friends, misled by that temporary closeness after his son-in-law's murder and my own brush with death last summer.

"I'm sorry, Ruthie. I did mean to race over and apologize for sounding as if I didn't have confidence in you," Michael said, "but I've been tied up." I intercepted a glance at Patricia as he spoke. "I should have realized what you're going through and been to see you sooner."

"I wasn't expecting a knight in shining armor to rescue me," I said.

"And I'm not trying to play that role, but Denise is right. I can call other pharmacies and see what we can learn."

Ten

I stared at Michael, feeling my face flush. "That's not necessary," I told him. "I can do it myself."

Michael hesitated. "It's better if another pharmacist makes those calls." He spoke slowly, as if he were choosing his words carefully this time instead of rushing headlong into conversation the way he usually did.

"Why?" I asked but suddenly understood what Michael hadn't wanted to say. If I were unable to clear myself and went to trial—either civilly for accidental substitution of one drug for another or criminally for deliberate substitution—making such calls myself might be incriminating.

The others seemed to realize I now knew what Michael had left unsaid. "We need to discover as much as possible about anyone closely involved with Amy Brookman," Denise repeated.

"I suppose we can look up each of their addresses and call pharmacies in their neighborhoods."

"Let's also try to find out where they work. Perhaps they drop off prescriptions on the way in or on the way home." This was Patricia's suggestion, and I thought it sounded like a sensible one.

"We can do better than that," Denise said. "I'll talk to Jeremy Douglas, Amy's uncle. The one who works for Food Go. I'm sure he can give us addresses and workplaces for most of Amy's family. And maybe for other people—like her boyfriend."

"I'll be happy to coordinate the list and look up all the telephone numbers," Patricia offered.

Michael smiled at her. "If this weren't so serious, I'd say it sounds like we're planning an amateur show."

I decided it was time to tell them about the attorney I'd consulted. "I should talk to him before we go ahead," I said.

We agreed that I would contact Sterling Harraday and call Michael at his daughter's house as soon as I got the lawyer's advice. Meanwhile, Denise would try to save time by seeing Jeremy for the information we wanted from him.

Patricia and Michael refused more coffee. They left, first reassuring us that they would stay in close touch. I stood in the doorway with Denise and watched them cross the two driveways to Betsy Stokes's house.

"That was unexpected," Denise said.

I couldn't pretend to misunderstand. "We never made any commitments."

"Obviously *he* didn't," she said drily, "but what about you?"

Gathering up the dirty coffee mugs, I walked quickly into Denise's kitchen with them. My ploy to avoid discussing Michael and Patricia didn't work. I hadn't thought it would.

"Ruthie, if you really care about Michael, you'll have to fight for him."

How typical of Denise, I thought. She was scripting scenes from an old movie for me to play out, determined to link Michael and me romantically although she had no idea we'd dated all those years ago. Denise was a good friend, but I couldn't talk about the time back in pharmacy college. And who today would believe that our love had never been consummated?

I wanted to tell Denise to follow her own advice, not to give up so easily when she met someone she liked—but I would never hurt her that way. Instead I tried to deflect any suspicion that I was interested in Michael.

"Patricia seems like a very decent person."

"Very attractive, if you like skinny intellectual types."

My laughter was genuine. "Intellectual?"

"Didn't you notice her way with words? And her suggestions were very clever."

"Patricia did seem intelligent," I agreed. "I'm glad Michael's found someone like her. He's had enough problems."

"Everyone has problems," Denise said. "Speaking of which, let's get to the store early so I can try to question Jeremy."

I put the mugs in the dishwasher while Denise replaced the leftover cookies in their original box. Yes, I thought, you have a lot more to worry about than Michael taking another woman to meet his daughter. But it hurt to know he had someone else.

I remembered my own visits to the house next door. When I first knew Betsy, I'd stereotyped her as a "dumb blonde," a gold-digger, who had married an older man for his money and was after Michael even before her husband's funeral. Later, knowing her as Michael's daughter, seeing how vulnerable she was, and realizing she had loved Harry Stokes, my attitude changed. Now, whenever I saw Betsy, I could think only that she might have been my daughter if Michael and I had married, but I couldn't admit any of this to Denise.

She didn't pursue the subject. Instead, on the way back to my house to pick up my car, we went over the information she would try to get from Jeremy Douglas. "What do I say if he wants to know why?"

"Tell him the truth, Denise."

"I wasn't going to lie."

"Sorry, I didn't mean it that way."

We were stopped for a red light at Camelback and Hayden, and Denise turned to look at me. "You've really been hit hard from too many directions at once, haven't you?"

"I can cope," I assured her. Privately, I wasn't so sure. Although I'd made a determined effort to avoid self-pity after the first shock of widowhood, sometimes the battle still raged. These days, it was escalating to all-out war. My resistance had been lowered by too many sleepless nights since Amy Brookman's death. Now, despite the discovery that any fantasies about Michael were just that, I couldn't afford to feel sorry for myself. I must concentrate on clearing my name. If Patricia and Michael were willing to help, that was all that mattered.

Denise dropped me off. The morning had been so debilitating, I felt I needed a quick shower and change of clothes before starting on my late shift at the pharmacy. Something bright, I thought, as I looked through my closet. I didn't want to look defeated.

I chose a floral print in shades of rust and gold. Once I arrived at the pharmacy and put on my white jacket, no one would see the dress. Customers would glimpse only the top third of my body when they approached the pharmacy window with their prescriptions, but I could look down and see the cheerful colors whenever I needed comfort.

The pharmacy was busy. Louise looked up from the computer screen when I came in. "You can take over here," she said by way of greeting. "And I'll get the people at the window."

Why did my staff pharmacists always want to displace me as pharmacy manager, I wondered. Louise had changed during the last two weeks, acting almost as if I were incompetent and she must guide me. I still found it difficult to be assertive but knew I must force myself before things got completely out of hand.

"That's okay, Louise," I said. "I'll get the window." Before she could answer, I quickly grabbed my white jacket and walked over to help the first customer in line.

She was a short, dark-haired young woman who handed me a birth-control prescription. It was a new one, not a refill, and I passed it to Louise to enter into the computer while I went to the shelves to find the Ortho Novum. When the paperwork emerged from the printer, I started to place the label on the hinged lid of the compact but noticed the customer was trying to get my attention.

"I forgot to ask how much it will cost," she said.

I looked down at the computer-generated receipt. "It's $19.65."

"So much!" She seemed dismayed. "I don't know if it's worth it."

Just then, as if on cue, we heard a child howling elsewhere in the store. We grinned at each other. "I guess it is worth it," she said.

It was the kind of incident that made me enjoy my profession. Even today, with all the unshakeable worries in the forefront of my mind, I found myself smiling again as I helped the next customer. He was a middle-aged man who came in for a Zantac refill every month but never had the vial or the prescription number.

"Number?" I asked, although I already knew the answer.

"It's in the computer."

"Okay, I'll look it up and fill that for you, sir."

He turned away but came back to the window before I reached Louise at the computer. "Isn't my Zantac ready yet?" he asked.

"Sir, we need to look it up and make sure you still have refills. Then we'll try to get you out as soon as possible. So give us about fifteen minutes." Instantaneous service would be wonderful, I thought, but even if he were the only customer in the place, it would still take time to fill his prescription.

I could see there was no way I'd have time to call Sterling Harraday. Louise's shift was due to end soon, and it was Karen's day off. Once Louise left, I'd be busier still. In any case, I didn't want her to overhear my conversation with the lawyer. I'll wait until tomorrow, I decided. I would be opening up and could surely find time to make the call.

The rush of customers continued. Louise suddenly walked away from the computer and removed her white jacket, signaling that she was ready to leave. "Mrs. Jackson will be in later, but we never got an okay to refill her Ventolin inhaler," she told me.

"Couldn't you reach her doctor?"

Louise shrugged. "He's been out all day."

"All right. I'll explain it to her. Anything else I need to know before you leave?"

"No, but there's something I'd like to ask."

She probably wants to exchange hours with me, I thought. Tim, my previous staff pharmacist, was always reluctant to swap when I needed to change shifts, but I'd be glad to oblige Louise. I waited for her to continue.

"Have you heard anything more about that mistake?" she asked. "Are they going to prosecute you?"

I should be beyond shock at Louise's bluntness, I thought, but couldn't repress a shudder at her callous words. She could easily have framed the question differently, something like "I hope that nonsense about the so-called mistake has been dropped." Maybe that was wishful thinking, though. Louise seemed to believe not only that I was capable of making such an error but also that I had done it. I couldn't understand her attitude. From the beginning, when she first came to fill in at Food Go, I'd tried to be friendly with her. But she had remained aloof.

Louise would make a great witness for the prosecution, I thought unhappily. Well, I would just have to prove that she was wrong. Even Michael, who had seemed unsupportive when I first told him about Amy Brookman's death, was now actively trying to help. Although it hurt to find that someone else now had Michael's love, I told myself it was more important to learn that he did believe in me after all.

Louise was staring at me, tugging on her long braid, large dark eyes unreadable. She waited expectantly, looking older than her twenty-three years, more like the cartoon figure of a woman ready to hear a juicy bit of gossip over the back fence.

"There was no mistake, Louise," I said as firmly as I could.

"You can't just wish it away."

"I'm saying that I made no error."

Louise didn't even try to hide her disbelief. "Well, I hope you have a good lawyer," she called over her shoulder as she left the pharmacy for the day.

Surprisingly calm, I continued to help my waiting customers. This time, I didn't have to depend on the years of professional experience to carry me through. I knew I had friends who believed in me even if my staff pharmacist did not. Buoyed by this knowledge, I worked on, feeling more like myself than I had for some time.

This precarious self-confidence got an unexpected boost from my next patient, a young woman who dropped off an amoxicillin prescription for her nine-year-old daughter. When she returned to the window, I had the antibiotic ready. "You probably know the school nurse can't dispense anything unless it's fully labeled," I said. "Would you like another label and a small vial for her to take to school?"

"What a great idea!" she said. "That way, Michelle won't have to bring the entire bottle back and forth every day."

I attached a second label to an empty vial and added it to her package.

"That's really thoughtful of you," the woman said. "I can't tell you how much I appreciate your help."

I suppose I could have called my attorney instead of taking time for this woman and for some of the others who needed extra attention that afternoon, but Dad had taught me well. Patients need that little human touch, and I wasn't going to neglect my professional responsibilities no matter what happened.

The evening went by quickly as I tried to keep up with periodic customer rushes and do paperwork during any slight lull. I didn't have much time to worry about my situation but did wonder why I'd heard nothing from Denise. It was impossible for me to take a break and walk into the coffee shop since I was alone in the pharmacy. The waitresses, on the other hand, had regularly scheduled breaks, and I kept expecting Denise to come by and tell me what was happening.

I knew the meat cutters began work hours before we did. Maybe Jeremy had an early shift today. Or he could have the day off. No point guessing. Denise would surely let me know as soon as she had some information. Closing time came, however, without any word from her.

When I left the store, though, I found Jeremy waiting just outside the doors nearest the pharmacy end of Food

Go. "How's my favorite pharmacist?" he said, but the words sounded forced this time.

"Fine," I assured him. "Is everyone okay at home? I can reopen if you have a prescription."

"No, I don't need anything." He hesitated for a moment, fiddling with the bolo clip on his western tie. "Denise caught me as I was leaving this afternoon."

"I knew she planned to talk with you."

Jeremy spoke as if he were measuring his words. "I wasn't sure if it was okay to give all those names and addresses out. But after I got home from work, I thought about it all evening. And I talked it over with Lupe."

I waited, trying not to think how much depended on Jeremy's cooperation.

"We decided it was better to make one more try first. I mean to get the family to drop everything."

"The lawsuit?" Even if they dropped the civil action, I still needed to find out what really happened in order to clear my name.

He nodded. "You saw that I couldn't convince my brother—Amy's father. But it's really his wife, ex that is, who's pushing the lawsuit. And that boyfriend of hers smells money, so he's egging her on."

Two customers, pushing a grocery cart, passed us on their way out of the store. They nodded to me and looked curiously at Jeremy. Although I was one of the most visible Food Go employees, the meat cutters were rarely seen by customers. I knew they were wondering about him and our earnest conversation.

Jeremy also noticed their interest. He waited until they passed out of earshot. "We can't talk here," he said. "Why don't you follow my truck? I want to take you to see Leila."

My earlier self-confidence plummeted at the thought of meeting Amy Brookman's mother. If she were anything like her sister, Virginia, I was in for a terrible time. A rapid mental argument followed my first "can't do it" reaction. You know you didn't cause Amy's death, I told myself. Let's not revert to that scenario. This is your opportunity to know more members of the family. And Jeremy could be right. Maybe we can change his sister-in-law's mind.

"Okay," I said. "Let's go!"

He showed me where his pickup was parked and walked me to my car. I eased out of my space and waited just behind his parking spot until he pulled out.

Why didn't I take down the address, I wondered as I followed. What if I lose him? Jeremy drove slowly, however, carefully waiting after each stop sign and traffic light to make sure I got through. Traffic was thin at this hour, and his white pickup was easy to follow.

We drove about twenty minutes before pulling into a driveway on the Scottsdale side of the Indian reservation, just west of Pima Road. The neighborhood was a modest one, negating the common assumption that only wealthy people live in Scottsdale. I couldn't see much of the house in the dark, but its white exterior and avocado trim looked freshly painted.

Jeremy had emerged from the pickup and walked back to my Honda. I let down the driver's window, suddenly afraid to leave the comfy blanket of my car. "Does she expect us?" I whispered.

In the dim light from a street lamp at the corner, I could see his embarrassed expression. "I couldn't take a chance on calling, Ruthie. She might have told me to go to hell."

This was getting worse by the minute. Leila Brookman didn't sound like someone who would listen to reason. I sat there, ready to back up and flee.

"I'm trying to help," Jeremy said.

He was right. If I wanted to stop the threat to my self-esteem and professional reputation, I had to take advantage of this opportunity. I got out of the car and followed Jeremy to the front door, trying not to hang back too noticeably as he rang the bell.

A harsh voice, male, called out, "If you're selling something, we don't want any."

Oh no, I thought, but forced myself to ignore the impulse to run. Jeremy, undaunted, gave his name in a firm voice. When the door opened, he nodded encouragement and pushed me gently forward.

The man framed in the entry light was not as tall as

Jeremy but looked like someone who worked out regularly. Muscles bulged below the sleeves of his purple and orange Phoenix Suns T-shirt, and I thought if he decided to throw us out, even Jeremy couldn't stop him.

"Who is it, Nick?" a woman's husky voice called out.

"Your brother-in-law and some broad."

"My ex-brother-in-law. And don't call Lupe a broad. You're as bad as Quentin."

He muttered to himself as he led us through a cluttered family room into the kitchen. I didn't catch anything he said, but from the tone was glad I couldn't hear the words. "It ain't Lupe," he said as we walked into a brightly lit kitchen that must have been a holdover from the sixties. Everything in it was avocado green—appliances, counter tops, linoleum, and curtains.

Leila Brookman didn't look at all the way I'd pictured her from Jeremy and Lupe's comments. I guess I expected someone flashy and brassy. Leila, however, except for the obvious age difference, resembled her sister. Like Virginia, she was tall and thin, with the same well-shaped features. The similarities ended there. I had only seen Virginia twice but both times, she wore dark suits with white blouses. Leila was casually dressed in black T-shirt and checked slacks. The main difference was her facial expression. Even when Leila frowned at Jeremy's introduction of me, she showed none of Virginia's grimness.

"What do *you* want?" she said, but it was as if she were reading lines in a bad play. The words had no force.

"And this is Nick Kenmore, Ruthie," Jeremy continued blandly, as he nodded toward our escort.

Nick's scowl was more intimidating than Leila's words. I dug my heels into that avocado linoleum and stood fast.

"If you've come to apologize, forget it," Leila said. "It won't do any good."

"No, I didn't come to apologize. I'm sorry, of course, that your daughter died, but I had nothing to do with it."

"Let's go sit in the front room," Jeremy said. No one paid attention to him. We remained in that avocado kitchen, under bright fluorescent lights and glared at each other; that is, Leila and Nick glared at me. I tried to look concerned (the easy part) and relaxed (the impossible part).

"Why did you bring her?" Leila asked Jeremy.

"I want you to listen to her story."

"Story is right," Nick said. "I'll bet it's a good one."

"Just give Ruthie ten minutes," Jeremy pleaded.

"Sure thing. It's your five million we're going after, so talk."

"Five million! I don't have five million."

This confrontation was completely different from anything I'd expected. Instead of trying to convince them of my innocence, I was now sidetracked by sheer incredulity at the magnitude of their claim.

"You got that kind of insurance that the doctors have," Nick said.

"You mean malpractice insurance? But pharmacists don't carry large amounts like that."

"Well, the supermarket can make up the difference."

I looked at them, not understanding for a moment. "You didn't tell me you're suing Food Go, too," Jeremy said. "You know I work for them."

"So what! They won't go out of business because of one lousy lawsuit. Every company gets sued these days."

Their greed made them seem like ambulance-chasing caricatures. Surprisingly, after my first incredulous reaction, their preposterous claim fortified my resolve. "You have no case," I told them. "Neither I nor Food Go had anything to do with Amy's death."

Nick moved closer, invading my space as he hovered over me. "We don't have to prove anything. All the jury needs to hear is how Leila lost her beautiful daughter. They always side with the little people against big companies."

"Ruthie isn't a big company," Jeremy said. "You're going to ruin a decent person's life just to make some money. Blood money!"

"We deserve that money," Leila told him. She moved closer to Nick so that both of them hemmed me in.

"No, you don't," Jeremy said. "Amy couldn't even bear to live with the two of you."

Nick's voice turned ugly. I ducked involuntarily as he raised his fist. I had already noticed the black and blue marks on Leila's arms and didn't want to be his next victim. "And just what are you trying to say?"

Jeremy became the peacemaker again. "Let's sit down and talk this over like sensible people," he said. Without waiting for an answer, he took my arm and propelled me away from Leila and Nick to a wrought-iron chair at the kitchen table. He seated me and pulled out another chair for himself. "I could use some coffee," he said to Leila. "We are guests here, even though I admit we weren't invited."

He must have known how to deal with his former sister-in-law because she smiled and busied herself with a jar of instant coffee. She filled four cups with tap water and put them in the microwave. All of us waited without speaking until the coffee was ready. The coffee was bitter. Everyone else that I knew used bottled water or had a reverse osmosis system to filter the terrible-tasting city water. I was grateful for the coffee, though, realizing for the first time how much this confrontation was affecting me.

Leila and Nick seemed an odd couple. Each time they started to fit one stereotype or other, something shifted. I had expected Nick to pull a can of beer out of the refrigerator, but he drank coffee with the rest of us. And Leila certainly didn't seem like a grieving mother. Not only because she wanted to profit from her daughter's death, but also because she showed no signs of sadness. I thought of her sister, Amy's aunt, who had seemed shattered by the girl's death.

I remembered another murder last summer. The parents had been inconsolable, wanting to talk nonstop about how wonderful their son had been. Leila, on the other hand, still hadn't said a word about her daughter.

The four of us sat at the table, making the coffee last, as if reluctant to begin speaking again. It was Jeremy who returned to the subject we had come there to discuss.

"The reason I brought Ruthie here, Leila, is that I wanted you to see what kind of person she is. She's a good pharmacist. Real professional. Helps people all the time, like she helped when we couldn't get that medicine for Manuel. What you're trying to do is gonna ruin her."

He paused, eyes fixed on Leila, waiting for her to react. For a long time, she said nothing. Then she turned to me.

"Look," she said. "I'll level with you. I got nothing personal against you. Maybe you made a mistake and maybe you didn't."

"I didn't!" I said with as much energy as I could muster.

"That don't matter. I'll bet you got a nicer house than this. Well, you're my ticket outta here. I'm gonna have a house in Paradise Valley. And I'm gonna shop in Saks and Neiman Marcus." She smiled dreamily at Nick. "And Nick wants a boat, so I'm gonna buy him one."

I couldn't believe what I was hearing. She was admitting things that would damage her in court. As if she read my mind, Leila said, "And don't think you can tell the judge what I just said. I'll deny it all, and Nick will be my witness."

Eleven

I looked at Jeremy. Didn't Leila realize he could corroborate what we heard here tonight? She followed my glance.

"Jeremy's still family," she said. "When push comes to shove, he won't forget Amy was his favorite niece."

"Don't be so sure I'll back you," Jeremy contradicted.

"I am sure."

"I can't let you treat Ruthie this way. Not when you just admitted you're deliberately going after the deepest pockets."

Leila stared at him and then at me. "I never knew you liked older women," she said. "Tell me, does Lupe know you got something going here?"

Even though I realized the purpose behind her ridiculous accusation, I could feel my face flush. She grinned at me. "Well, why not? He's a handsome guy. I got to admit, I always liked him better than Quentin. After it was too late, anyways."

Nick slammed his fist into the kitchen table so hard he rattled the coffee cups. "Stop fooling around, Leila. I'm not gonna tell you again."

This wasn't getting us anywhere. It was definitely time to leave. I turned to tell Jeremy I wanted to go, but the doorbell interrupted me. Now what, I wondered.

Leila said the same words aloud as she went off in the direction of the front door, returning with a thin, dark-haired boy who looked about fourteen years old. "Hello,

Tommy,'' Jeremy greeted him, and I realized he must be Amy's boyfriend.

I saw Nick's face harden as he looked at the boy. ''What do *you* want?'' he asked. ''Didn't we tell you not to come around here no more?''

No one answered Nick, but Leila had walked over to the kitchen counter and was already filling another cup with instant coffee and tap water for Tommy. I glanced at him curiously, knowing from Jeremy that the boy was older than he looked—seventeen, in fact—and that he'd wanted to marry Amy.

Jeremy, in that easygoing way of his, asked Tommy how he was getting along, while Nick glared at each of us in turn. Leila, at least, could keep occupied. She motioned to the boy to take her own seat, brought over the cup of coffee for him, and resupplied the rest of us. Despite the negative, greedy side that I'd just witnessed, I had to admit Leila was a conscientious hostess to all her uninvited guests.

''Who did you want to talk to?'' Jeremy asked.

The boy fidgeted in his seat, without answering. He was wearing a blue flannel shirt and unfrayed jeans, his light brown hair neatly combed. Either he worked at a place that enforced a dress code or had taken care with his appearance before coming here.

''Yeah, what *do* you want?'' Nick repeated.

''Amy's mom.''

Leila looked surprised but told Nick to let the boy have his coffee in peace. She went and stood behind Nick's chair, her hands massaging his shoulders. He made no move to offer her his seat or to bring one from elsewhere in the house. It was Jeremy who rose and said he'd get another chair from the master bedroom.

Tommy gulped down his coffee so fast that he must have scalded his mouth. ''I think about Amy every day,'' he said suddenly.

For the first time that evening, I detected a trace of sadness on Leila's face. ''So do I,'' she told him. I could see the sudden tightening of the hands that had been caressing Nick's shoulders and the corresponding strained look on his face, but there was no way to tell whether he was feeling sympathetic or annoyed.

Jeremy returned carrying a brass stool by its rim, three legs protruding outward. It was the kind some women used with their dressing tables or bathroom vanities. Under one arm, he gripped a cushion—the color we used to call hot pink. He put the chair down next to Leila and carefully replaced the round cushion. She nodded her thanks but remained standing.

Tommy cleared his throat a couple of times. "I've been watching the house most nights," he said to Jeremy, "trying to see Amy's mom alone. But *he's* always here, and I was afraid to come in."

With a quick movement, Nick started to get out of his seat. Leila pushed him back and even though he could easily have shaken her off, he subsided. "Sure, I'm always here. I live here."

"You must go out sometimes," Tommy said. "I've been waiting for days." He looked toward Jeremy again. "Then, I saw the two of you arrive tonight, and I figured he couldn't do anything to hurt me while you're both here."

"Hurt you, you creep. You'll be lucky to get out of this house alive." This time, Leila couldn't restrain Nick. He jumped out of his chair and rushed to confront Tommy. The boy leapt from his own seat and turned to Jeremy for protection in a scene that would have been farcical if the situation were not so serious.

Now Jeremy was out of his chair, too, blocking Nick. "Are you crazy? Leave the kid alone. He's got a right to talk, and I want to hear what he has to say."

Tommy seemed too frightened to speak. "I'm leaving," he said. "You gotta let me go."

"Don't worry, kid. No one's going to hurt you."

"He's going to kill me, like he killed Amy."

Leila looked stunned. I think Jeremy and I shouted at the same time, asking Tommy what he meant. The surprising part was Nick's reaction. I expected him to make a more determined effort to get at the boy and shut him up. Instead, he sat down again and laughed.

"You think this is funny?" Jeremy asked.

"Sure, I do. The kid don't know what he's talking about. This ain't the first time he's been saying things against me. Why do you think I told him to stay away from here?"

"You didn't tell me about it," Leila said.

"There wasn't nothing to tell."

"Then why was he watching the house? Why is he here tonight?"

They stood, arms folded, glaring at each other, voices harsh—in complete contrast to the loving tableau they had presented only a few moments before. "I didn't want you to hear his lies," Nick said.

"You let me be the judge of that."

"Can't you see he's got some crazy idea in his head? He's just looking for someone to blame because Amy wouldn't marry him."

"Why would he blame you? You didn't try to stop them from marrying."

Nick softened his body language and his voice. "Look, honey. Let's throw everyone out. We don't need to talk in front of them."

I waited, expecting to be ejected along with Jeremy and Tommy, thinking it would be more dignified to leave first. Never having met Leila or Nick before, I couldn't assess the likelihood of being thrown out, so I watched Jeremy, figuring he knew these people. He made no move to go, so I settled back in my chair. After all, more than anyone else, I needed to know what Leila and Nick were up to and whether Tommy had real knowledge of what happened to Amy.

A rapid exchange of meaningful looks followed. Leila seemed upset, but Nick continued as the voice of reason. "You just got over the bad time, honey." He spoke to her seductively, as if they were alone in the room. "Let's not start all over again just when you been doing so well."

She moved forward and leaned into his body. "Okay, I guess you're right."

"Don't let him con you the way he conned Amy," Tommy cried out.

"Shut up and get out."

"You think you can scare everyone because you lift weights. I know you're twice as big as I am, but so's he." He pointed to Jeremy. "I pleaded with Amy to go to him for help. See your uncle, I told her, but she was afraid. And now she's dead."

I wondered how much of the boy's words came from his grief over losing Amy and how much could be true. There didn't seem to be any motive for Nick to kill her. She didn't even live with her mother and Nick.

"She's dead because you couldn't keep your hands off her," Nick said.

Tommy choked back a sob. "That's not true. I loved her; I wanted to marry her."

"That's your story."

"What's the use of talking about it now?" Leila asked. "It's too late."

"You have to know what really happened. You have to know what kind of man you live with."

"Wait a minute," Jeremy said. "I don't get it. Why are you blaming Nick?"

"You don't understand."

"Then tell me."

"I said to get out!" Nick shouted.

"And I want to hear what the kid has to say," Jeremy countered. I said nothing, still wanting to run but unwilling to miss what was happening.

Tommy spoke to Leila. "Mrs. Brookman, I don't want to hurt you . . ." He hesitated, seeming to search for the right words, as she turned to face him.

"Shut up!" I thought Nick's rage would frighten the boy into silence, but it had the opposite effect this time.

"It was his baby," Tommy said.

I sat there frozen for long moments before I could look at the others to judge their reactions. Leila's mouth was open in a wordless "Oh," and I saw Jeremy move quickly to block Nick from going after the boy.

"That's a damn lie," Nick bellowed. "You're just a troublemaker."

"It's the truth, and you know it." Tommy appealed to

the rest of us. "Why do you think she couldn't bear to keep the baby? Or even to let you have it," he said, turning to Jeremy.

"I always wondered why she wouldn't marry the kid," Jeremy muttered, half to himself. He seemed to be turning Tommy's words over in his mind, trying to pinpoint their accuracy. Suddenly, he made his move, grabbing Nick's T-shirt with both hands and facing him down.

"It's bad enough when it's two kids who think they're in love. But if I find out you went after Amy, a sixteen-year-old, for God's sake . . . I'm gonna kill you." He released Nick's shirt and turned toward his former sister-in-law.

"And you, Leila. Her own mother. You must have known what was going on." He didn't touch Leila but looked murderously at her, too.

"That's why she went to live with her Aunt Virginia," Tommy said. "She couldn't stand being in the same house with him."

Leila looked as if she, too, were weighing the boy's words. "Nick . . . ?"

"Damn it, Leila. You know me better than that. You're not gonna believe this punk."

"Why did she move out?"

"She was restless, you know that. Remember how she moved in with Quentin for a while."

Leila seemed relieved. I could see that she wanted to trust Nick.

"I knew he'd talk you around." The boy's tone was anguished. "That's why I was trying to see you alone."

It was hard to come to grips with what I was hearing. I wanted to get out of there and take the time to sort things over in my mind. If Tommy's claims were true, it would put an entirely new slant on the pregnancy that led to Amy's death. But how could anyone prove or disprove his story?

Twelve

Tommy had made two accusations against Nick: that he had impregnated Leila's daughter and then, that he had killed her. If the first charge were true, the second could have resulted from it. Suppose Amy threatened Nick. She was only sixteen; he was more than twice her age. Not only would such an accusation have ended Nick's relationship with Leila but, since Amy was underage, it also could have led to prosecution and a long prison sentence.

Although it was obvious that Jeremy wanted to stay and shake the truth from Nick, Leila abandoned her hospitable manner, urging us to go, insisting she would find out what really happened.

"Okay," Jeremy agreed. "I'm leaving it up to you for now, but I won't drop this."

"Don't worry. I won't drop it either." Leila looked hard at Nick.

"Come on, kid," Jeremy said. "You'd better come with us."

"Just a minute." Leila grabbed the boy's arm to get his full attention. "Tommy, if it turns out you just wanted to make trouble, you'll have to deal with me."

"It's the truth, Mrs. Brookman. Amy made me swear not to tell anyone, and I kept my promise all this time. But I couldn't stand it anymore. I had to tell." He walked behind me and just ahead of Jeremy to the front door, using us for protection. I could sense his fear, and I was frightened, too.

When we reached the door, I pulled it open, hurrying onto the front walk to escape this house as quickly as possible. But Tommy stopped in the narrow entry and, blocked as he was by Jeremy's large frame, shouted at Leila and Nick.

"She didn't have to die. I won't let him get away with it."

Jeremy propelled him out through the doorway and into the cool October night. For a moment, I recoiled inwardly, expecting Nick to come barreling after us; but there was no sound at all from the house, and the only acknowledgment of our presence was a negative one. Before we had taken more than a few steps along the front walk, the outside lights were switched off and we were in darkness. Again I felt that touch of fear, knowing how many Arizonans are proud gun owners. Maybe Nick was planning to shoot at us. No, I reminded myself. We would have made better targets with the lights left on.

Tommy had parked about half a block away from the house. We walked him to his car, an old blue and white Colt, and waited while he unlocked it and climbed in. He rolled down the driver's side window. "What I said," he told us, "was true. I couldn't make up a story like that."

Jeremy stood there, seeming to think things over. "How did you find out?"

"She told me. We never . . ." He hesitated. "I knew it couldn't be my baby." His voice became an anguished cry in that quiet street. "We loved each other. She wasn't seeing anyone else. Then he came along."

"When did she tell you?"

To me, it sounded like Jeremy was pressing for more details because he doubted the boy's story. I didn't know what to believe, but I had a sickening feeling that Tommy was telling the truth.

"Not when it first happened. She just got very quiet and kind of sad and went straight from school to her aunt's house one afternoon. She didn't even try to get her clothes and stuff from her mom's. I couldn't understand it."

In the moonlight, I could see that Tommy looked uncomfortable. "I mean, her aunt was much stricter than her mom. We couldn't see each other on school nights any more and things like that.''

"Did she tell Virginia?''

"No, she was afraid to.''

"Well, what did Amy say to you? And why didn't she speak to me or her father so we could take care of Nick?'' said Jeremy.

I wondered if Jeremy believed him or whether he was leading the boy on to trip him up. Tommy remained silent for a few seconds.

"She was flattered and she was willing at first. Then when she tried to break it off, she didn't think anyone would believe her.''

"God damn it!'' Jeremy exploded. "At least we would have checked it out when she became pregnant. There's ways now to be sure. Blood tests.''

"Amy wasn't acting like herself. All she could think of was getting away from him.''

"We'll never get Nick to admit anything now,'' I said, surprised at myself for breaking into their conversation.

"Leila won't let it rest. If there's any truth to this story, she'll get it from him.''

"He certainly won't admit to murder,'' I said.

"Murder?''

"Yes, Jeremy. You're outraged that he'd seduce Amy. And I agree that's unconscionable. But think about it. If Tommy's right, he may have killed her.''

"What are you talking about?'' Jeremy asked. "I thought he meant that Nick was responsible for her death because the pregnancy was his doing.''

"And I think someone murdered Amy. If the baby was his, who had a better motive?''

Jeremy turned to Tommy. "Tell us exactly what you meant. But first, let's find someplace where we can talk without hanging out the car window.''

"I won't go back to their house.''

"Okay, I have a better idea. Quentin needs to hear this.''

"Amy's dad won't listen,'' Tommy said. "She didn't get along with him. He was too strict.''

Maybe nobody was strict enough, I thought, but didn't

say it aloud. I was nearly two generations older than Amy and Tommy, and I knew my views were different. If not, I might have been married to Michael all these years. And then again, I told myself, you would have missed your life with Bob.

Tommy agreed to drive to Quentin's and wait for us in front of his home. We backtracked to Leila and Nick's driveway, my nervousness increasing the closer we approached to their place. It was very quiet. Either their house was too solidly built to expose arguments or they had settled their differences.

"Do you think she believes Tommy?" I asked Jeremy. "Do you?"

"I don't know."

"That young man was terrified of Nick."

"He'd probably be as scared if he made up the story."

I thought about it. Maybe I was just looking for a way to clear myself. Yet, Tommy's story seemed to make sense. I wondered whether any of us were safe if Nick had deliberately killed Amy.

"Do you want to leave your car here and ride in the truck?" Jeremy asked.

I didn't ever want to return to this house, so I told Jeremy I'd follow him. We would have made a small cortege if Tommy had waited, but he had taken off quickly and was out of sight before we reached our own vehicles.

Quentin lived in an older condominium not far from his ex-wife's house. I pulled into a visitor's parking lot next to Jeremy's truck and looked around. Although the landscaping featured desert plantings, tall palm trees and salmon-colored oleander bushes gave it a lush appearance. As I got out of my car, I noticed that Tommy's Colt was already in the lot.

"Leila got the house when they divorced," Jeremy told me when I reached his truck. "This condo is nothing fancy. He got just enough together to make the down payment."

"How can we drop in at this hour? Won't he be asleep?" Arizonans are early risers. People think nothing of telephoning at seven in the morning, but apologize for calls after nine in the evening.

"I don't care if he is asleep. This is important."

"Well, he's your brother."

"Half-brother," Jeremy corrected. "Listen, he's got no complaints. I'm the one who has to be at work early tomorrow."

I said no more but it was now after 11 p.m., and I was still dubious about arriving unannounced at this hour. Tommy joined us at the front door of a one-story condo that, from the outside, seemed to be all garage. We could hear chimes echo through the house, but no one responded to the doorbell. Jeremy rang again, holding his forefinger on the bell. This time, a voice thick with sleep sounded through the door.

"Who the hell's there?"

"Jeremy."

"What the hell do you want?"

It wasn't an auspicious beginning. And he didn't know that Tommy and I were there, too. Not for the first time that night, I wished I were safely at home. I took a deep breath and steeled myself for what was to come. Too much was at stake to worry about Quentin's reaction to our visit.

"I hope you've got some clothes on," Jeremy said. "I'm not alone."

"Hold on a minute."

We waited at least five, but Quentin finally opened the door. He grunted a greeting to the other two but just stared in my direction. I could see he didn't remember me.

Quentin led us to his living room, flopped into a brown recliner that took up a good part of the small room, and grunted to us to sit down. The place had an untidy look, with clothes and copies of USA Today strewn around the floor. There was a green sofa that looked like a Salvation Army reject, and not much other furniture.

I brushed aside some of the mess and, without waiting for an invitation, cleared enough space for Jeremy and myself to sit on the sofa. The cushions felt uncomfortably hard, and there were no throw pillows. I figured Leila must have gotten most of the furniture.

Tommy pulled over a rickety-looking folding chair and sat across from us. We certainly wouldn't get any hospitality here, I thought. But I reminded myself I wasn't there for coffee.

No one spoke for a while. "Well, you must've had a reason to come and wake me up," Quentin said finally.

"I don't know how to tell you this," Jeremy said. "Maybe you should just listen to what Tommy here has to say."

"Well, spit it out, kid." Quentin obviously didn't have a clue to what was coming.

"Tommy, tell him what you told us over at Leila's," Jeremy prompted.

"You're coming from there? What's going on?"

"Just listen, Quent. We need your advice."

"That's a new one."

Tommy looked as if he wanted to get up and run out of the house. I could sympathize with him. "See, everyone blamed me," he said. "But Amy and I never did anything."

"Say what you mean," Jeremy told him. He turned to Quentin. "The boy claims they never made out. That it was Nick's baby."

Quentin zoomed out of the recliner so fast I couldn't suppress a scream. He grabbed Tommy, yanking him out of the folding chair so forcefully that it tipped over. "Is that the truth? Are you telling me the truth?" He didn't wait for an answer. "I'll kill that miserable animal. And Leila, how could she let him touch our little girl?"

He suddenly let go of Tommy and collapsed on the floor, turning away from us as he wept, gasping and wheezing in a futile effort to control himself. I saw Jeremy start to go to him and then change his mind. We waited, not making eye contact.

After a few minutes, Quentin got up and left the room. He returned with a bottle of Jim Beam and some paper cups. "Here, we can all use this."

"Tommy's underage."

"What are you, a cop now?" There were no end tables or coffee table in the room, so he sat on the floor, pulled

over a sheet of the discarded *USA Today,* and put the whis-
key and cups on it. We all joined him, sitting crosslegged
on the floor, and helped ourselves. No one spoke.

The alcohol did help. At least it kept me from giving
up and running ignominiously out the door. Quentin
started to speak, stopped, and began again. "Tell me what
you know," he said to Tommy.

"She was acting so strange those last few weeks. Crying
all the time. And she wouldn't tell me why." The boy
stared at the floor as he spoke. "Then after she moved to
her aunt's, she wouldn't hardly talk to me."

"If it wasn't your baby, why was she mad at you?"
Quentin asked.

"She wasn't just mad at me. It was everyone and mostly
herself. Maybe I'm not explaining it right." He suddenly
looked up toward me. "Do people get like that when
they're depressed?"

"Maybe. If they feel they have no control over their
lives."

"That's it," he said. "She kept telling me she couldn't
go on. Couldn't face things, is how she said it."

I hated myself for the surge of hope, but I couldn't help
it. They say soldiers on the battlefield feel this way, sad
for the ones who died but unable to control the joy of
survival. It sounded as if Amy had committed suicide, and
that would exonerate me.

Jeremy was the one who pursued the idea. "Are you
saying that Amy killed herself?"

"No. She said she thought about it but couldn't do it.
And then she told me what happened." He helped himself
to some of the Jim Beam, grimaced as though he wasn't
used to alcohol, and continued. "We were sitting in the
park over near the high school. She was crying so hard, I
couldn't understand her right away. I wanted to beat Nick
up, but I knew I didn't stand a chance with him."

"Why didn't you come to me?" Quentin demanded.

"She didn't want anyone to know. I told her it wasn't
her fault, but she kept blaming herself. She said she should
have moved out when he started coming on to her. But at
first she was flattered; she thought it was really love."

Quentin got up and paced around the tiny living room, nearly knocking over the bottle and cups. "And where was her mother? Why didn't Leila help her?"

"Amy and Nick got together back in August, that time her mom went to San Diego for a few days to cool off. He said he had some kind of deal in the works and couldn't leave town, so Amy's mom went by herself."

"That selfish woman," Quentin yelled and pounded his fist on the wall. He stood there, massaging his reddened knuckles, seeming unaware of what caused the pain.

"Stop it, Quent," Jeremy said. "Leila couldn't know what would happen. And she doesn't even believe it. Right this minute, Nick's probably talking her around."

"She loved her daughter," I said. "Anyone can see that."

For the first time, Quentin Brookman seemed to notice my presence. "And who the hell are you?" he asked. He turned to Jeremy. "Why is she here?"

"This is Ruthie. You know, the pharmacist."

"What?" he bellowed, and I was afraid he'd take his rage out on me. "Are you crazy, Jeremy? She's the one who killed Amy."

"Now just sit down and listen to the rest of Tommy's story," Jeremy said. "He thinks Nick killed Amy to keep her quiet."

I expected another explosion from Quentin, but he said nothing at all.

"She was afraid of him. He said he'd kill Amy if she told anyone it was his baby."

"It does make sense in a way." Quentin spoke very slowly. "It explains why she refused to marry Tommy and why that old battleaxe, Virginia, was so enraged."

I thought of Amy's aunt that day at the pharmacy. She did look grim, but so do many relatives of the young women who come in after a miscarriage. This morning at the demonstration—was it really only this morning?—she certainly seemed implacable. On the other hand, I told myself, she didn't come across as an opportunist like her sister. If Virginia really believed me responsible for her niece's death, I couldn't blame her for those dour looks.

"If you want me to take a lie detector test, I will," Tommy suddenly said.

"You've been watching too much TV, kid," Jeremy told him, not unkindly.

"Well, what do you think?" Quentin asked his brother.

"I don't know."

"That makes two of us. I've got half a mind to go over there now and take Nick apart."

"You won't get anywhere with him. He's too slick," Jeremy insisted.

"Well, I'll get somewhere with Leila," Quentin said. "I can always tell when she's lying to me."

"That's assuming she knows."

"I'll give her a day or two. If there's anything to find out, she'll know by then."

Quentin walked over and grabbed the boy's arm in a gesture almost identical to Leila's earlier in the evening. "And you, Tommy, if I find out *you're* the liar . . ."

"I just don't want him to get away with what he did."

"You stay out of it now," Quentin said. "I'll take care of the two of them."

Thirteen

Quentin spoke with such icy force, I was nearly as frightened of him as I'd been of Nick. I looked at Jeremy. He seemed the only rational one I'd dealt with that night. Yet, I knew he and Lupe had cared about Amy, too.

We didn't stay much longer, and I was glad to leave all of them. Reminding myself that Jeremy was not the only one with an early shift the next morning, I slid into my car to drive home.

After all the confrontations that evening, and despite my weariness, I anticipated an uneasy night with little or no sleep. Exhaustion took over, though, the moment my head hit the pillow.

I don't know what I expected the next day. All the threats that were voiced the night before made me jump every time the telephone rang. And in a busy Food Go pharmacy, the phone is seldom quiet. I worried about Tommy. He was the only one with direct knowledge about Nick and Amy; he'd make a prime victim. Maybe I should warn him, I thought, and realized how ridiculous that would be. I didn't even know how to reach him, and I couldn't bring myself to ask Jeremy.

Nothing relating to Amy Brookman or her family happened during the next few days. I would be off on Sunday and Monday this week, and I wanted to phone Michael to see if he had new information. Good excuse, I told myself. You know he'd call you if he learned anything. Probably too busy with Patricia, I thought, and wanted to kick myself for succumbing to the old self-pity bug that I'd worked so hard to exterminate after my first months as a widow.

On Sunday, Patricia called me. Her telephone voice was low and throaty, but with a sparkle to it. I guessed men would consider it sexy. "We were planning to see the duck race yesterday," she said, referring to an annual fund-raising event during which tens of thousands of rubber bathtub ducks are launched into a Scottsdale canal. Each duck has a paying sponsor, and the sponsors of the fastest rubber ducks are awarded prizes.

"But Michael had to drive back to Tucson," she continued. "Something about the relief pharmacist coming down with a twenty-four-hour virus."

"Oh," I said, thinking my response didn't sound very bright. If someone were recording this conversation, Patricia would win hands down in the personality department. Then I reminded myself I wasn't in competition with Patricia. I had let Michael go too many years before.

"He's been calling every pharmacy contact, and he planned to keep trying from Tucson." She paused. "Most important, Michael wanted me to get your schedule for tomorrow; he expects to be back up here in the morning."

So why didn't he just call me and ask, I wondered. Don't be a fool, Ruthie. He wanted to talk to Patricia. Why make two long-distance calls? I resolved again to restrain feelings that kept getting in the way of the more pressing issues at stake.

"Tomorrow's my day off," I told Patricia.

"Terrific! When and where would you like to meet?"

"Can you come here? Any time that's convenient for both of you."

We made an appointment for eleven the next morning, subject to Michael's arrival from Tucson in time. "But he said he'll probably be here tonight," Patricia told me.

Sure, I thought. He won't want to miss spending the night with you. And I couldn't blame him. She was everything I was not—sophisticated, elegant, cosmopolitan. I knew I envied her, but I liked her, too.

Since I'd been trained to be meticulous in my father's pharmacy, my house was always neat. I vacuumed the carpets, anyhow, and went to the nearest supermarket for some pastries. Patricia's probably a world-class baker, I thought, and gave myself another mental kick for regressing.

I spent time carefully choosing my clothes for the next day, rejecting any silk dresses first of all. It wouldn't do to look overdressed. Besides, with a sunny and warm weather forecast, we might sit out on the patio. Slacks, I decided, stifling the image of Patricia Donleavy in her well-tailored beige slacks and cream blouse. My hair had lost much of its natural ginger color and I now depended on my hairdresser, but I was no more than five pounds over my college weight. White slacks with a black and white striped blouse would do. They'd look neatly crisp, just right for a visit that really wasn't a social call.

Too bad I couldn't control my thoughts as easily as I did my wardrobe. For months now, I'd been denying how much Michael meant to me. Now, even though Patricia would be with him, I couldn't ignore the soaring feeling, the anticipation that always took over when I knew I'd be seeing him.

Monday morning, they appeared promptly at eleven. I suggested the patio, and they both agreed. Patricia also wore white slacks, but her blouse was cocoa, which set off her blond hair. She stretched out on one of the padded lounges and sighed. "This is heavenly. But I mustn't relax too much. We need to be serious."

Michael laughed. "When are you ever serious?" He'd taken one of the white wrought-iron chairs around the table, partially shaded by the turquoise umbrella I'd made sure to open that morning. He was wearing khaki pants with a navy and khaki shirt. The combination looked great on him.

I did my best to be a gracious hostess, but they waved away offers of refreshment. "Maybe later," Michael said, pulling out a chair for me next to him. "Let's not get distracted now. There's too much to discuss."

"You found out something?"

"Not enough, Ruthie. But we can build on it."

I tried to hide my disappointment. After all, what could

I expect in just under a week. They had their own lives to lead.

"Since you couldn't get much information from the girl's uncle, we had to work with whatever I was able to pull up."

"We may be able to get more cooperation from Jeremy after all. I'll tell you about it later."

"First thing I did, I ran through all the connections I've built up with other pharmacists over the years—people I know from continuing education seminars and state conventions." He paused, as if unsure that he wanted to continue. "Some of them were concerned about the ethics of revealing patient information, the way you were when I needed to know about Harry's prescriptions."

I understood his hesitation, remembering how he had reappeared in my life after the death of his son-in-law, Harry Stokes. I'd refused to give Michael the computer printout he wanted to help prove his daughter hadn't killed Harry.

"After I explained," Michael continued, "I did get some results."

I was shocked. "You told them about the accusations against me?"

"No, of course not. I just gave a general picture without using your name or revealing where you work."

"Why don't you tell Ruthie exactly how you went about gathering information?" Patricia said.

His expression showed his approval of her suggestion. "By the way, Patricia stayed up and organized my notes last night. She started a database with all the material I was able to gather."

"A database?"

"You know, a list of every pharmacy I called, the telephone number, the contact person, and brief remarks about what they did or didn't tell me."

"I know what a database is, Michael. I was just surprised."

"It didn't take long," Patricia added, as if she wanted to downplay her contribution. "I have a laptop computer with me."

I smiled at her. "Thanks, Patricia," I said and realized I meant it. She was a stranger, but she believed in me.

"What I did," Michael said, "was list every pharmacist I know personally. Especially the ones who work for chains. I figured they'd have access to the records of patients who fill their scripts anywhere in the chain."

"And they were willing to divulge prescription information?"

"Well, I went about it as indirectly as possible. First I had to get the right person. Some of them were actually off for the weekend."

I laughed despite my tension. It's a standard complaint of pharmacists that we often have to work nights, weekends, and holidays.

Michael continued, telling me that he knew at least one pharmacist in each of the chains. "The first one I called refused to give me any patient information, so I changed my tack. From then on, I began by saying that I only needed to know two things."

"Two things?" I echoed.

"Yes. Was so-and-so a patient and was he or she taking Coumadin?"

"Didn't they ask the reason?"

"Some did. I told them I wasn't at liberty to say."

"And they bought that?"

"Ruthie, you have to realize these are pharmacists who know me. They understand I wouldn't ask for information idly. I suppose they figured it involved some kind of court case, but they don't know about you."

"Not to sound ungrateful, Michael, but how can it help me if you contact pharmacists in Tucson?"

"That's why I started with the chain stores. Their computers are networked, so they can punch in the patient's name and check chainwide."

"I can't believe I didn't think of accessing Food Go's computer database," I said.

"No problem. You can hit theirs on your next shift." He removed a neatly folded sheet of paper from his pants pocket. "I listed everyone I could think of—her mother and father, Leila and Quentin Brookman . . ."

I interrupted Michael. "Didn't the other pharmacists recognize the name Brookman?"

"If they did, they never said anything."

Patricia, silent until now, spoke up. "When people aren't directly involved, they usually don't remember things like that."

"Then there's Lupe and Jeremy Douglas."

"Oh, no," I said.

"We have to consider everyone," Michael insisted.

"But Jeremy's been helping me. That's part of what I want to talk to you about later."

"He could be helping you to avoid raising suspicion against himself, Ruthie. Let's keep him on our list, along with the others—the aunt, Virginia Rowland. The demonstrator you told me about, Faith Sommers. And Amy's boyfriend, Tommy."

"There's one more person we didn't know about," I told him. "Leila Brookman is living with someone."

"Nick Kenmore," Michael said.

"How did you know that?"

My astonishment seemed to please him. "There are some surprises left in the old boy."

"Indeed!" Patricia said.

I tried not to look disconcerted, but her smile, quickly concealed, seemed too knowing. This was no time to get sidetracked, I told myself. It was more important to hear the details of Michael's investigation.

"Were any of our suspects taking Coumadin?"

"Only three of them shopped at the chains I called so far, Ruthie. Neither Faith Sommers nor Nick Kenmore filled Coumadin scripts."

"They could go to other pharmacies for that particular drug."

We both knew that was possible. Many people shopped around for prescriptions just as they comparison-shopped for other commodities. Besides, stores often offered promotional coupons for as much as ten dollars off new scripts. At Food Go, we tried to counteract this trend by accepting any other store's coupons. I sometimes griped about the bother of transferring prescriptions from store to store for people I privately considered to be "coupon abusers."

I felt discouraged. With more than three million people in the Phoenix metropolitan area, which includes Scottsdale, Phoenix, Mesa, Tempe, and other adjacent cities, I didn't see how we were going to find out which of our suspects had access to Coumadin, the blood thinner that Amy Brookman shouldn't have taken.

Patricia seemed to sense my mood. "Couldn't you try the uncle again, the one who works at Food Go? He may know who has to use Coumadin."

"You mentioned three people. Who was the third one?" I asked.

It was getting warmer now as noon approached. Michael shifted his chair into the shade. "Patricia, would you like something cold to drink? You're not used to this climate."

"Water would be fine."

My impatience to hear about Michael's discoveries had to wait while I went into the kitchen and took down a turquoise enameled tray from the top shelf in one of the cabinets. I stifled the realization that I hadn't used this tray since Bob's death. Quickly filling two pitchers with crushed ice, I added the iced tea I always kept on hand for myself to one of them and filtered water to the other. The tray was too heavy now, so I removed the pitchers to carry them out separately, placing napkins, silverware, plates, and a platter of small pastries on the tray.

I carried the tray out first, planning to return immediately for the two pitchers. As I approached the sliding french doors to the patio, I could see Michael and Patricia framed through them. He had moved from his seat at the table and was perched on the edge of her chaise. Leaning toward her, in earnest conversation, he was unaware of my return. I imagined I could almost see the charged air between them.

For a moment, I had to move away and put the tray down. I couldn't bear to go outside and face the two of them. Although I'd been warning myself that Michael felt only friendship for me now, this scene put everything into perspective. I realized, even with Patricia's arrival, I hadn't abandoned romantic images of the young Michael and Ruthie on the campus in Tucson all those years ago and my hope that we could somehow recapture those days. Didn't I occasionally read such stories in newspapers and magazines? Couples who had been separated in their youth and eventually found each other again to live happily ever after.

I smiled ruefully. Did I really believe in that sort of destiny for myself? It was more important to think about saving my professional reputation. Michael's private life hadn't been my concern for more than thirty-five years, and it was pointless to allow regret to take over when I needed to direct all my energy to discover what really happened to Amy Brookman.

Gathering up the tray again, I balanced it on one arm and slid open the patio doors. I carefully set the tray on the table, my eyes deliberately avoiding Michael and Patricia. Then I went back in and reemerged with the two pitchers. This time, I found that Michael had returned to his seat at the table. I busied myself passing around beverages and pastries, trying to appear unruffled.

Michael chugged down a full glass of ice water before continuing his story. "Faith Sommers gets her scripts filled at Walgreens," he said. "No Coumadin. Nick Kenmore and Leila Brookman are both Osco customers. No Coumadin for him." He paused and delivered the next bit of information in staccato tones that only served to underline their importance. "Leila Brookman is on Coumadin, one tablet, 2 milligram strength, every other day."

"Two milligrams," I shouted. "Those are the purple ones."

"Let's not jump to conclusions," Michael said. "You know as well as I do that Coumadin is heavily prescribed."

"And if Nick Kenmore lives with her, he'd have access, too," Patricia reminded us.

"I could believe it of him. He looks like a thug."

"That doesn't make him a killer. What about motive?" Michael asked.

I remembered that Michael and Patricia knew nothing about my visits with Jeremy. It was time to fill them in. "If anyone had a reason to kill Amy Brookman, it was Nick," I finished.

"That's not enough to convict anyone. It's not even enough to try him."

"What a horrible man!" Patricia said.

"Not only that, but I'm sure he abuses Leila. She had bruises . . ." I stopped. "Of course," I said.

They both looked surprised but waited politely for me to continue.

"Nick seems like such a brute that when I saw black and blue marks on Leila's arms, I made the wrong assumption."

Now Michael's face registered understanding, but Patricia still looked bewildered. "Coumadin is prescribed for people with heart conditions," Michael explained to her. "It's a blood thinner, and when the blood is thinned, people bruise very easily. So it often causes black and blue marks on their arms and legs."

"But Leila seems young to be taking Coumadin," I said.

Michael looked thoughtful for a moment. "Consider the dosage," he said. "Every other day sounds like there's a family history of heart disease. It was probably prescribed as a preventive measure."

I nodded agreement. "It does give us something to work with."

"Too dangerous and too soon."

"I have to act. Do you expect me to just sit and wait for a civil or criminal action against me?"

"No, of course not. But we haven't checked everyone out. Wait until you look up all of our suspects in the Food Go computers."

"I didn't recognize any of them as Food Go customers."

"What about Lupe and Jeremy Douglas?"

"You can't suspect them!"

"Ruthie, be realistic. We have to suspect anyone connected with Amy. Anyone who could have switched her medications.''

''What about the young man?'' Patricia asked. ''Perhaps his parents are patients of yours even if he's not.''

I hadn't considered Tommy's family either. I remembered that a few months ago, someone I thought I knew had come close to killing me because I hadn't suspected him until it was nearly too late. If I were to gather enough information to take to the police, I must not be so trusting this time.

Fourteen

My schedule, odd for most people but typical for pharmacists, put me on the night shift Tuesday after my Sunday and Monday off. I came in early to have lunch in the Food Go coffee shop. Denise was standing at a corner table, order book in hand, talking to a customer. She was wearing one of her most becoming outfits—a multicolored lavender, violet, and orchid skirt with a long-sleeved orchid blouse. The weather was still warm by tourist standards, but most Arizonans had put their summer things away.

Denise's expressive face seemed to glow, and I looked more carefully at the customer. Dark-haired, slightly balding, horn-rimmed glasses—my attorney, Sterling Harraday. Denise didn't notice me, but Sterling gestured to the empty chair at his table. I saw her face fall and then brighten when she realized who was joining Sterling.

If only she's not hurt again, I thought, as I walked up to them. Denise's happy-go-lucky attitude masked a vulnerability that I'd become aware of only recently. Stop worrying about Denise, I told myself; she's friendly with all of her customers.

"Mrs. Morris," Sterling said, pulling out a chair for me. "You're just the person I wanted to see."

"Can I get iced tea for you, Ruthie?" Denise asked.

"Please. And my usual tuna on rye bread."

She turned to go, but Sterling stopped her. I read anticipation in her face and wondered if she expected him to invite her to join us. "Could you top up my coffee, please?" he said.

"Yes, sir. Right away." I could see the light go out of her eyes, and her voice was toneless. It seemed I hadn't imagined her interest in the lawyer. Thinking of Michael and my own disappointed hopes, I ached for her.

"I was in court most of the morning," Sterling said, "but I was planning to call right after lunch and fill you in."

Denise returned with the coffee pot in one hand and a tall glass of iced tea in the other. Sterling waited until she put the tea in front of me, refilled his coffee, and walked away. "I had a call yesterday from an Eric Manning, the attorney for Amy Brookman's family."

"Yes, I heard of him. He's a cousin of theirs."

"That's not the issue here," Sterling started to say, sounding pompous for a moment. Then he laughed at himself. "Sorry," he said. "I tend to forget that things may seem important to my clients even though they don't really affect the case." Now, I could see something of his appeal for Denise.

"I guess I'm the one who should apologize," I said. "You're the expert in this area, and I need to rely on your judgment." I waited, wanting to tell Sterling of my own findings, but knowing I should hear him out first. He paused, sipping his coffee, but I was too nervous to touch my iced tea.

"They haven't filed a civil suit yet," Sterling said. "It seems they're willing to settle out of court for . . ." He broke off as Denise returned with my tuna salad sandwich.

"It's okay," I told him. "Denise is a close friend of mine. I don't have anything to hide from her."

He looked surprised, and I wondered if he was one of those people who couldn't see beyond Denise's waitress job and the frilly green apron that hid the front of her colorful skirt. If he were, Denise might as well take her daydreams elsewhere, I thought. And then I remembered that mine would never materialize either.

Despite my assurances, Sterling waited for Denise to

walk away before continuing. "They're asking for $250,000," he told me.

"That's absurd," I said.

"You do have malpractice insurance," he reminded me quietly.

"I didn't commit malpractice."

"But you need to consider all the possibilities. No one can predict how a lawsuit would turn out."

"Why are they suddenly willing to settle for $250,000? They were talking about millions."

"I gathered that they don't want to wait for the money. If we agree to settle now, they won't file the suit. So unless there's a criminal action—and I very much doubt there's enough evidence to get an indictment—you're home free."

"You don't seem to understand," I said. I tried to match his quiet tone, holding my indignation in check. "Settling would mean admitting I gave Amy the wrong medication."

"Not settling will mean publicity first of all. And once it goes to court, anything can happen."

"I realize that," I said. "But I can't do it. They just about admitted they're only after money." I told him about my visit to Leila's house and the conversation there.

"Will the girl's uncle testify in your behalf?"

"I don't know," I said, miserably.

"We have to consider that they may be right about his attitude. Family loyalties can be overwhelming."

"But that isn't the point," I insisted. "I'm sure now that Amy was murdered, and they're claiming I made a mistake to cover it up and also to get some money out of the situation."

He listened without interruption while I recounted the rest of last Wednesday evening's events. "I'm not trying to talk you into settling with them," he said when I had finished. "You're the one who'll have to make the final decision. But I'd be remiss if I didn't present the pros and cons."

"Do you think I have enough to take to the police?" I asked.

He paused so long this time that I nearly repeated the question. "That might be wise, after all. Would you like me to accompany you?"

I tried to think whether I'd look guilty if I brought along my lawyer, but I didn't know enough about the way the system worked. I'd have to go by instinct, and my instinct—or maybe it was my fear, which had returned tenfold—insisted I'd be safer with Sterling at my side.

We were both unavailable the next day, but we agreed to try for Thursday morning. I told Sterling about Detective Moreway and how I'd helped find his young brother-in-law's murderer. "For a while, he suspected me," I said. "But I think he knows me better now."

"I'll have my secretary make an appointment for us," Sterling said. He picked up my check and his own, left a three-dollar tip for Denise, and walked away. Despite my own turbulent emotions, I watched to see whether he'd take the opportunity to talk to her. Instead, I saw him pay the cashier and leave the coffee shop without a backward glance.

Denise approached my table a few minutes later, saw the three dollars, and winced. "I wish they'd abolish tipping," she said.

"Then they'd have to raise salaries."

"Most of the time, I don't mind because the money comes in handy and Lord knows, I work hard enough here."

I looked up in surprise. Denise never complained. "I know it's easy for me to say, but don't take it personally," I told her.

"But it is personal sometimes. He had a sandwich and coffee. You had a sandwich and tea. This is only a coffee shop, not the Phoenician. A normal tip would have been about two dollars, but he threw in the extra dollar just because we talk a lot."

"Denise," I started to say and stopped abruptly.

"I know," she said, holding up her hand. "I'm being foolish, but he's the most interesting man who comes in here."

That was a side to Sterling I hadn't noticed, maybe because I only cared about his competence. "Are you on break yet?" I asked. "Can you join me for a bit before I have to check in at the pharmacy?"

She went behind the counter to tell her manager she'd be taking a break and returned to sit at my table, first removing the green apron to show she was off duty. I gave her all the news as quickly as I could.

"Then that settles it," she said.

"We'll find out when your friend Sterling and I meet with Frank Moreway."

She made a face at the word "friend." "Maybe you're satisfied to be Michael's *friend*," she said, emphasizing the last word, "but I'm looking for something more than friendship."

"We don't always have much choice."

"No, not if you just give up."

"I'm not giving up. I just told you we're going to get the police to investigate Amy's family and whether one of them murdered her."

"I wasn't talking about Amy Brookman, and you know it. If you really care for Michael, you have to fight for him."

"You know we're . . ."

"Yes, I heard all that before. But I don't believe it, and I'm sure you don't believe it either. Betsy let slip that you and Michael were going together way back when."

I kept forgetting that Denise and Michael's daughter were neighbors. "I was twenty years old then. That ended a long time ago."

"Only if you want it to be over."

"Denise, please don't dramatize. This isn't a soap opera."

She started to laugh. Denise didn't exactly giggle, but her laugh had an infectious quality that always made me join in. "It's sure beginning to sound like one. Will Ruthie and Michael get together again after thirty-something years apart? Thirty-something. Now there's a good title."

"That's not what it means."

She ignored my comment. "Will the handsome attorney

realize that the waitress with the heart of gold is meant for him?''

I joined in. ''Will the police find the real murderer of sixteen-year-old Amy before our dedicated woman pharmacist loses her professional standing and goes to trial?''

We were both nearly doubled up with laughter. I suppose it was the release of tension because I realized now that some people did believe in me. And I knew I was ready to act to counteract accusations that had haunted me for weeks.

''Denise, your break was up five minutes ago.'' The coffee shop manager stood over our table, frowning at us. ''Maybe you think it's funny to keep people waiting, but I don't.'' For the first time, we noticed an older couple who had come in and taken a table at the far end of the room.

Denise jumped up, said she'd see me later, and put her apron back on. I watched her rush over to wait on the people, reflecting that even though my customers could be demanding at times, at least I wasn't accountable to anyone else in the pharmacy.

I had reason to remember that after I signed in and put on my own insignia of service, the white jacket with the name tag, RUTH KANTOR MORRIS, PHARMACY MANAGER. My staff pharmacist greeted me with an injured tone. ''I was hoping you'd get here earlier today,'' she said. ''It's very busy.''

I found myself making excuses about the things I'd had to take care of. Then, looking at my watch, I discovered my shift didn't actually begin for another twenty minutes. I turned to tell Louise, but she was at the window, helping a customer.

Why is she so antagonistic toward me, I wondered. Everyone else seems to believe in me now, but Louise still thinks I made a mistake in filling Amy Brookman's prescription. I hoped I would soon prove she was wrong to doubt me.

My first customer drove all thoughts of my own problems away. She was a blonde in her late twenties with a prescription for 100 Tylenol #4 with one grain of codeine and another for sixty Valium, 10 milligrams. That seemed excessive to me, so I looked more closely at the scripts. The physician was in Las Vegas. I tried to call him but found it was his afternoon off. The office was closed, and I got his answering service, so I left a message for him to return my call to check the dosages.

My instincts screamed "drug abuse," and I looked up to see where the patient was. She stood about ten feet back from the pharmacy window watching me. When she caught my eye, she returned to the pharmacy. "Is there a problem?" she asked.

I decided to ask her for an ID. "It's not for me," she said. "It's for my grandmother."

Trying to make it sound like routine, I insisted on seeing her driver's license. "But I'm paying cash," she said.

I never find it easy to lie, but something seemed wrong here. "Yes, but for out-of-state prescriptions, we need to see IDs."

She seemed startled, which didn't surprise me. "Oh, okay. It's out in my car. I'll be right back."

Now I knew. Over the years, the only patients whose driver's licenses were "out in the car" never returned. A phony prescription was the only explanation.

Louise had finished with her customer and heard this last exchange. "What in the world is wrong with you, Ruthie? I think that girl's death has affected your ability to deal with customers."

For a moment, I stood still, unable to answer her. Why couldn't I get a staff pharmacist who believed that my years of experience meant something? Why couldn't I get someone who looked up to me as a mentor? Why couldn't I at least get one who treated me as an equal? I smiled to myself ruefully, knowing I was not alone in facing what I thought of as careerism. Even in this pharmacy, one of the least busy in the Food Go chain, with only two full-time pharmacists, the number two person wanted to replace me as manager.

The thought made me smile in earnest. My job must be better than I'd realized if Louise wanted it so badly. I forced myself to speak casually. "Watch," I said. "Maybe you'll learn something."

I knew I sounded smug, but I felt it was deserved when fifteen minutes and then a half hour went by without the customer returning. "This is the way it works, Louise. If you suspect a phony script and you stall or do anything out of the ordinary like I just did, they fade away as quickly as the Cheshire cat."

"But you should report phony scripts," she said indignantly.

I might have known. How could she be so self-righteous at her age? "I had no way of being sure until she disappeared. I couldn't reach the doctor."

She turned away and, since both phones were ringing, I didn't pursue the point. We were both too busy to talk much after that. The few hours that we worked together flew by until it was nearly time for Louise to leave for the day. As she walked to the back of the pharmacy to hang up her white jacket, someone approached the window and began tapping on the counter. I hate when customers do that and looked up, trying not to show my annoyance. It was Jeremy Douglas.

"Ruthie," he called. His voice was hoarse and when I got closer to the window, I saw how haggard he looked. So that's it, I thought. He needs some medication in a hurry.

"Aren't you feeling well, Jeremy?"

"It's not me," he said.

Either Lupe or the little boy must be sick then. I should have realized he'd be more impatient for his wife's or son's needs than for his own. I waited, expecting him to hand me some scripts. He just stared at me.

"What can I do for you?" I asked to break the silence.

And big, teddy-bearish Jeremy put his hands over his eyes and silently wept. I reached across the pharmacy window and awkwardly patted his shoulder. Louise had come up behind me, wearing her own denim jacket now instead of the white pharmacy one. I knew she was ready to leave for the day, but curiosity had probably drawn her back to the front counter.

"Come on now, Jeremy," she said. "You'll scare away the paying customers."

Doesn't that woman have any empathy for other people, I wondered. But even as I stood there, wanting to respond angrily, her remark had its effect. Jeremy slowly brushed his hands away from his face.

"I don't know why these things are happening to our family," he said.

"What things?" Louise asked.

Jeremy looked at me. "Ruthie knows," he said. "First my sixteen-year-old niece got pregnant and had a miscarriage. Then she died. And we found out the father was . . ." He stopped, unable to say what we had learned— that the father was her mother's live-in boyfriend.

"Did the police arrest Nick for Amy's murder?" I asked. "Oh my God," I blurted suddenly. "Surely her mother didn't blame Amy and kill her for it."

"No, the one thing we know for sure is Leila didn't do it." His voice broke when he mentioned her name. My thoughts took another leap. Could Jeremy be in love with Leila? I quickly reviewed their behavior toward each other that night I'd met Leila. He had brought the chair for her when Nick hadn't cared enough to bother, but surely that was just Jeremy's polite way of doing things. On reflection, I couldn't believe Jeremy felt anything other than family loyalty toward his former sister-in-law.

"How do you know?" I asked.

The hoarseness in his voice was even more pronounced, and I could see how red his eyes looked. "Because someone murdered Leila this morning," he said.

Fifteen

At least two of our phones were ringing, but I ignored them. I could hear Louise gasp, but I fought to stay calm. "What happened?" I asked Jeremy. "Was it Nick?"

"I don't know. The police just notified Quentin, and he called me." He started to cover his eyes again but quickly forced his hands away from his face with an abrupt gesture. "I'm going over there now, but I thought I should come by and tell you first."

"Why would the police call Quentin?" I asked. "Aren't Leila and he divorced?"

"No, not really. We say so in the family because it sounds better now that Nick's living with her. Quentin and Leila are legally separated, not divorced."

"I know you want to be with your brother. But Jeremy, before you go, could you just tell me how she was killed?"

"Quentin said they won't be sure until after the autopsy. What it looks like. . . ." He stopped, and I could see his throat move as he swallowed hard before continuing. "They found the chair from her dressing table lying next to her. The police think she was knocked unconscious with it first and then choked to death."

I could picture that pink-cushioned brass stool and felt the blood draining from my face. What an awful way to die. Then again, any murder was horrible.

"I'm not sure I understand," Louise said. "Are you talking about the mother of that girl, the one who died from the wrong post-miscarriage medication?"

Jeremy gave an almost imperceptible nod, turned without saying another word, and walked rapidly out of the Food Go supermarket. Louise stared after him. "I must say that was rude. After all, he does work here with us."

Yes, I thought to myself. And you and I work together, too, but that doesn't stop you from rudeness even though you have less provocation. Aloud, I said, "Have a heart, Louise. She was his sister-in-law. You can't expect him to stand around and gossip with us about her murder."

"I never gossip." She barely paused before she said slowly, as though underlining each word, "Well, it's certainly good news for you."

This was a new low, even for Louise. I was appalled. "I don't know what you mean," I said, although I was afraid I knew exactly what she was driving at.

"The family'll be too tied up in knots to think about suing you now."

Before I could form an answer, she tossed her braid over one shoulder, picked up her purse, and left the pharmacy. I wanted to run after her, to convince her that I felt terrible about Leila's death, that any advantage to myself had never occurred to me. Both phones were ringing now, however, and a patient had just stepped up to the window.

I told the white-haired gentleman that I'd be with him in a minute and picked up each receiver in turn, asking the customers to please hold. Then I returned to the window, took the man's two prescriptions, promised I'd have them ready in twenty minutes, and went back to the phones. There was no time at all to think about Leila Brookman's murder.

Several times during the evening, the prescription rush quieted enough for me to visualize Leila as I'd seen her less than a week ago in that bright avocado kitchen, playing hostess to her unwelcome trio of guests. I pictured the brass stool from her vanity for a moment and shuddered, not wanting to carry the image further and think about the way Leila had met her death. Toward eight o'clock that night when business slowed longer than usual, I remembered Louise's words. It wasn't that they'd be too busy to consider suing me. This murder proved that something was wrong, something that had nothing to do with the prescriptions I'd filled for Amy Brookman. Saddened as I was by Leila's death, it represented one more piece of evidence to present to the Scottsdale Police Department on Thursday.

As if my thoughts had conjured him, Detective Frank Moreway appeared at the prescription window. The last few times I'd seen him, he'd been cordial. Tonight, his manner reminded me of that time, only a few months ago, when he suspected all of us—myself, Michael, Denise, Michael's daughter—of involvement in a couple of murders and an attempted murder.

"Ms. Morris," he said. "I need to talk to you."

"Didn't my attorney make an appointment for us to meet on Thursday?"

"This can't wait for Thursday."

"Oh, is it about Leila Brookman?"

"And how do you know about that?" His voice was heavy with suspicion.

Not again, I thought, but explained it to him. "Her brother-in-law works here at Food Go."

"Yes, I remember him," he said drily. "The one who thought I was harassing you the last time you got mixed up in a murder investigation."

"I hope you're not implying I'm involved this time. I didn't even know the woman."

"You were at her house only last week."

"I didn't say I never met her."

"You're quibbling now," he said. "People usually don't invite casual acquaintances to their homes."

"She didn't invite me," I said.

He stared hard at me, and I realized how that sounded. For once, I was happy when the phone started ringing. "Excuse me, please," I said and went to answer it without waiting for his approval.

By the time I finished with the caller, two more customers were at the window. Frank Moreway looked at them and evidently thought better of continuing our conversation. "When you close up, I'd like to talk with you," he said. "I'll expect you at my office about nine-thirty tonight."

"I don't think I should see you without my attorney," I said, while the heavyset woman in bright red slacks and a red turtleneck, standing just behind Detective Moreway, leaned forward to listen.

"That's up to you," he said. "But I'm not waiting until Thursday."

"I'll try to reach him."

"You do that. But remember, nine-thirty sharp."

I glared after him, thinking of the private eye stories where the police always suspect the P.I. first, even after they've been proven wrong in case after case. You'd think by now he'd trust me, I told myself. And I'm not a private investigator, holding back information to protect a client. Then I remembered that I had once tried to keep things from him to protect Michael and Denise.

I took a prescription for Ortho-Novum 35's from the woman in red. It figured. As soon as they start thinking about bed, they remember they're out of birth control pills. She smiled at me. Actually, it looked more like a knowing smirk.

"You be sure to have your lawyer with you, dearie. Otherwise, your ex will keep it all," she said. "I just about let my old man get away with murder. But I know better now."

For a minute, the word "murder" startled me. Then, I realized she was using the term figuratively. If you only knew what I need *my* lawyer for, I thought. I smiled back as I handed the filled prescription to her. "Thanks for the advice." I nearly added "dearie" but stopped myself in time. Smart-alec answers did not go over well when serving the public.

I thought about her advice, misapplied as it was, while I finished with my final customer and began my closing routine. As I waited for the computer to print out a copy of that day's Rx record, I looked up Sterling Harraday's home telephone number and debated whether to call him. He probably wouldn't come out this late anyhow, I told myself. Besides, I had nothing to fear from Frank Moreway. It wasn't like the first time I'd gone to his office with computer printouts for everyone in the Stokes family and for Denise, too. Clearly, Leila's live-in boyfriend had killed her. None of my friends was in danger of being falsely accused of *this* murder.

I took off my white jacket, put it neatly on a hanger, locked the door to the pharmacy, and went to sign out as I had done thousands of times before. The sign-out process was so automatic after all these years, I rarely resented having to punch a time card. At Food Go, it didn't matter if you were a professional or a clerk. Everyone who worked for the supermarket chain signed in and out.

Pima Road was the best route to police headquarters on Via Linda, and I couldn't help thinking of Leila when I passed her street and hoped she hadn't known she was about to die. I pulled into the police headquarters parking lot at exactly 9:35 p.m. Not nervous this time, I congratulated myself, remembering how tense I'd been back in August.

Frank Moreway was waiting for me at the reception desk and led the way to his office without saying anything. This would have terrified me once, but I felt calm and relaxed, knowing that I had nothing to worry about now.

He motioned me to a seat in front of his desk but stood to the side, looking down at me. "Leila Brookman was about to ruin you professionally and financially," he said without preamble. "Is that why you killed her?"

I was so astonished, I couldn't say a word. When I recovered from the initial shock, I found I was angry rather than frightened. "What is this?" I asked him. "Every time you can't find a murderer, you accuse me."

"If you read the papers, you know we've had other murders since the last time I questioned you."

"Probably drive-by shootings. Even you wouldn't suspect me of those." I was surprised to hear my flippant responses. It wasn't my usual style, but I just couldn't take his accusations seriously.

He suddenly stopped hovering over me and sat down behind his desk. "Suppose you tell me why you visited Leila last Wednesday evening."

"You obviously have the whole story from someone else."

"I want to hear what you have to say."

"That's why my lawyer and I made the appointment to see you the day after tomorrow," I said. "Don't forget, *we* contacted *you*. We think we know why Amy Brookman was killed, and now I believe the same person murdered her mother."

I went on to tell him about Wednesday night in detail. He didn't interrupt until I got to the part about Tommy's charges against Nick. "Did Leila believe her boyfriend was responsible for the daughter's pregnancy?" he asked.

I winced at the phrasing. "I'm not sure. She didn't want to believe it, but after we all left and she had time to think about it, she may have."

"Had she contacted you since that night?"

"No."

"Did you call her or see her?"

"I never had anything to do with her before or after that evening."

"And what were you planning to do about the lawsuit?"

"Her lawyer contacted mine. He wants to settle out of court." I told Frank Moreway about the terms. "So you see, they knew I had nothing to do with Amy's death. They never hid their reasons for blaming me. They were after as much money as they could get from me and from Food Go."

"No one else has confirmed that part of your story."

So my lawyer was right about Jeremy. He was protecting his dead sister-in-law and wasn't going to talk about her greed. "It's true," I insisted.

"We only have your word."

"And my lawyer's. He'll tell you about the offer to settle."

"Which doesn't prove anything. People may settle for all sorts of reasons."

I looked at him—the neat navy-blue suit, the pale gray shirt, the darker gray tie. Then, I glanced down at his shoes. Once before, when I'd noticed he wore brown shoes with his blue suit, I'd realized he wasn't infallible. It had given me courage then to deal with his questions. Tonight, I wasn't the same easily intimidated person. Maybe it was because I'd outwitted a murderer and survived his attempt to drown me. Or it could have been because I was convinced Leila's murder, beyond any possible doubt, meant that I had not given Amy the wrong medication.

"Do you seriously believe I bashed this woman over the head and then strangled her?" I asked him. "And before you demand to know how I knew the way she was killed, let me tell you it was from Jeremy Douglas."

He didn't exactly smile then, but the crease between his eyebrows deepened and his lips turned up slightly. "I have to question everyone with motive and opportunity. You did have a motive. Now let's get to the opportunity part. Where were you since last midnight?"

"Home."

"Alone?"

"Of course. You know I'm a widow."

This time the smile was unmistakable. "You can't be that naive."

I don't often blush, but I could feel my face redden. Michael's image came into my mind so clearly it was almost as if he were in the room. Just think, I told myself, if you were having an affair with Michael, he could be your alibi. "Let's just say I was alone and forget the rest of it."

"Did you have any telephone calls? Anyone come to the door? Run any errands?"

The questions were thrown at me so fast, I barely had time to digest them. That was probably his intent, but since I had no reason to lie, I answered "no" to all of them.

"What time did you leave for work?"

"About eleven-thirty this morning."

"You work a nine-hour shift now?"

"No. I usually come in early when I'm on nights and eat lunch in the coffee shop. And today," I added, "at least two people can vouch for that."

"As you'll discover when you see the news, by that time, the police had already been called in."

He continued to fence with me for another hour, several times making me repeat the conversations of that evening at Leila Brookman's. Suddenly, he asked what I did after leaving Leila's house.

"Didn't anyone fill you in on our visit to her ex-husband?" I still thought of Quentin that way.

No response. So, I told him everything I remembered. He stopped me to ask whether I saw any indication that Quentin blamed his wife for Nick's actions. Although I was convinced Nick murdered Amy to keep her quiet, I thought carefully before answering. It was possible that Quentin killed Leila, but I didn't know of any reason for him to kill his daughter. It seemed highly unlikely to me that we had two murderers operating here.

All of this went through my mind very quickly but took longer to explain to Detective Moreway, especially since he remained skeptical. "On the other hand, *you* had a motive for both deaths," he said.

"Here we go again. Look, I don't mean to be flippant, but I know I didn't go anywhere near Leila or Leila's house except for that one time last Wednesday evening."

"Nevertheless, we do need to take your fingerprints," he said.

"I don't mind. But how can you tell when fingerprints at the house were made? After all, you know I was there last week."

"Were you in the master bedroom at all? Did you handle that chair?"

"No, of course not."

"Then you have nothing to worry about," he said.

Fingerprinting took only a few minutes, and I was soon on my way home. I couldn't stop thinking about Leila Brookman, though. Unlike the two murder victims last August, she was a relative stranger to me. Yet, I was involved with Leila and her family because of Amy and because of Jeremy and Lupe.

I had met Amy herself, her mother and father, and her aunt Virginia. Then there were Nick and Tommy, each of whom had accused the other of responsibility for Amy's pregnancy. More than that, I thought. Tommy believes Nick killed her. And I agree with him, but I didn't intend to do anything further about it. This time, it would be up to the police to identify the murderer.

I suddenly realized I hadn't told Detective Moreway about Michael's Coumadin discovery and decided that if our appointment for Thursday was still on, I could give him the information then. We no longer had to find out who had access to Coumadin. Now it was a job for the police. I wondered if Sterling would be upset with me for talking to them without him, but we could fix that on Thursday, too.

I didn't believe Frank Moreway seriously suspected me. If he did, I was sure the facts about Nick's possible access to the blood thinner should deflect him. I could think of no logical reason why anyone but Nick would have killed both women, and I realized now that my earlier suspicions of people like the demonstrator, Faith Sommers, were ridiculous.

My schedule called for an early shift the next day, but when I arrived home, I was too keyed up and too hungry to turn in right away. I found some of the pastries I'd bought to offer Patricia and Michael the day before and had two of them with decaf. Then, feeling very tired after all, I set the alarm and went to bed without even preparing my clothes for the morning.

When I hit the pillow, I deliberately avoided thinking about Leila Brookman's murder. Just before I fell asleep, though, a picture came into my mind of Jeremy carrying the brass stool from the master bedroom into the kitchen for Leila to sit on.

Sixteen

The image was still there when my alarm woke me at seven the next morning. This time, I realized its importance. Jeremy's fingerprints would be on the rim of that stool. I wondered if I should call and warn him. Maybe I'd wait and talk to him at the store. Then I realized Jeremy surely wouldn't be coming to work today. I must telephone, I thought frantically, and then decided it was too early. I would call him just before leaving for Food Go.

Lupe answered the phone on the first ring. Her voice sounded breathless and strained. "Jeremy. . . ."

"It's Ruthie Morris. From the pharmacy." Although I knew it sounded foolish, I couldn't ignore the conventions. "I was sorry to hear about your sister-in-law."

People usually make some kind of polite reply to such comments, but Lupe was silent. "I need to speak to Jeremy," I told her. "It's very important."

"I'm sure it is." She sounded so different, cold when she had always been friendly. "Well, thanks to you, Jeremy's at the Scottsdale Police Department, not here. They came to question him early this morning, and he had to go with them." Now her voice sounded as if she were trying not to cry.

"That's just routine," I assured her. "Detective Moreway questioned me last night, too."

"Really, and what did you say that made him come after Jeremy?"

131

"Nothing," I insisted. "I told Frank Moreway I'm sure Nick is the killer."

"Then why did they want to see Jeremy again? And why did they come for him instead of asking for a statement at his convenience like they did yesterday?"

I was too upset to conclude right then that Jeremy was probably the one who told the police about my visit to Leila's, leaving out essential facts like the purpose of the lawsuit. "Oh my God, Lupe. Did they say anything about fingerprints?"

"No, but they took his fingerprints yesterday."

"I know the reason for that," I said. "When we were at Leila's house the other night, Jeremy carried a brass stool into the kitchen for her to sit on." I could picture Jeremy as I described the scene to Lupe. "He had a three-legged stool in one hand and a pink cushion in the other," I told her. "It had to be the same brass stool the murderer used."

"It's pretty bad when the police can suspect a person because he was brought up to be polite to women."

I knew she was oversimplifying in her distress, but I didn't contradict her. "I'm sure he'll be home soon," I said.

"Why did you want to talk to Jeremy?"

"I wanted to remind him about what I just told you."

"So you put the police on him and now you're feeling guilty enough to want to stop them," she said.

"Lupe, it never for one moment entered my mind that Jeremy could murder anyone. And I certainly would never give the police any reason to doubt him."

"Not even to save your own skin?"

"My own skin is not in danger."

"It should be. We all know she was going to ruin you."

I was upset. Even considering Lupe's worry for her husband, it was an unpardonable accusation. "I don't understand you. Doesn't what Nick did to your niece bother you? Why are you blaming me instead of him?"

"Sorry," she said. "I'm upset right now. Deep down, I know it wasn't you and I'm ready to kill that animal myself." She was quiet for a moment. "Now if Nick had been murdered, any of us might have done it. Quentin, Tommy, Leila, Virginia, Jeremy, me. But why would anyone want to kill Leila?''

''That's why I'm so sure Nick did it. Maybe she confronted him. Said she was going to charge him with seducing her underage daughter.''

''I suppose that's possible,'' Lupe said, ''but Nick's not the type to stay around and wait for the police to pick him up. If he did it, he'd have drifted away.''

''Who found Leila?'' I asked.

''Nick.''

''Maybe he thought he'd look innocent that way—if he stayed and reported the murder.''

''That just doesn't sound like Nick.''

''Why wasn't he at work? Was Leila supporting him?'' Another minute and she'll tell me to mind my own business and hang up, I thought, but after a brief silence, Lupe continued.

''Nick's a mechanic. He *was* at work, but he had to take a car out to test drive. Something about a loud engine noise. He told us he forgot his lunch, so he figured he'd stop by the house and get it. That's when he found Leila.''

''And the police believe him?'' I asked.

''I don't know. Look, I have to get off the phone. What if Jeremy is trying to reach me?''

''I'll be at the pharmacy, Lupe. When Jeremy gets home, please ask him to call me.''

She didn't respond, and I heard the click as she hung up. I could only hope she'd give him the message. At least, she didn't ask why I wanted to talk to him, since it was too late for my warning. I wasn't sure myself. Certainly it wasn't idle curiosity—not when I was also a suspect.

I was going to be late opening the pharmacy, so I rushed off without trying to call Sterling Harraday. As soon as I finished my opening procedure, I'd try to contact him and let him know about last night's police interview. Unfortunately, three customers were waiting when I unlocked the door, keyed in the alarm code, and rolled up the metal shutter that protected the pharmacy.

My computer, which stayed on all night, was already

spewing out messages. I read that we'd be getting price updates early the next morning and that the pharmacies would be open only from 9:00 a.m. to 1:00 p.m. on Thanksgiving Day. Then I took the first of the prescriptions. It was a refill for E-mycin, acne medicine for the customer's son, a quick one to do.

The next patient was one of my favorite customers, a woman in her eighties who was always cheerful even though she was on Tamoxifen. I knew from her prescriptions that she must have had breast cancer because Tamoxifen is a maintenance drug to prevent recurrence of the disease.

"I need my poison," she said and smiled at me. It was a running joke between us. When she had first started taking the drug, she asked me whether there might be any side effects.

"Everything in here has possible side effects," I'd explained to her. "What we need to do is weigh them against the benefits."

"That makes sense," she said.

I gave her the package insert, the sheet that drug manufacturers must provide to give chemical formulation, usage, warnings, precautions, and so forth. Some doctors don't want patients to see the package inserts. I guess they're afraid people might develop side effects through power of suggestion or maybe decide not to take their medicine at all.

As I half expected, when I did reach Sterling Harraday, he was furious that I'd submitted to questioning without insisting on my right to an attorney. "But I know I had nothing to do with Leila's death," I said.

"That makes no difference. I can't look after your interests if you don't bother to contact me when something like this happens."

"I never expected to be treated like a suspect."

"Well, it would have occurred to me immediately. And I'd have kept the police from fishing expeditions."

"I'll bet Jeremy doesn't have a lawyer, and he's in more danger than I am." I told him about the meat cutter and how he'd handled the brass stool. "Maybe you should call his wife."

"I'm not an ambulance chaser. They'll probably contact Eric Manning." He paused and said in a matter-of-fact way, "This may stop the family from going through with the lawsuit."

I was furious. "Why do people think that way? This is much worse than a lawsuit. You have no idea . . . this woman . . . she was decent to us despite everything. I couldn't dislike her even though I wanted to."

"All right. I understand. But we have to be practical," he said. "Just before Manning's settlement offer expires, I'll call him. We should be able to get an extension in view of this death."

Callous as it seemed, I had to admit he was right. Nothing we did to fend off the suit would bring Leila back to life. "Are we meeting with Detective Moreway tomorrow?"

"I think it would be wise even though you seem to have told him everything we planned to go over."

The appointment was for 10:30 the next morning, and we agreed to meet at the Scottsdale Police Department. "And please follow my lead. I don't want you to answer anything that could be self-incriminating."

Again, I felt indignant. "If you don't believe me . . ."

"My beliefs have nothing to do with your legal rights," he said and ended the call with a polite reminder to wait for him before going into Detective Moreway's office.

Great, I thought. Now my own lawyer doubts me. I managed, however to maintain my new confidence and went about my work efficiently, filling prescription after prescription.

When Louise arrived to begin her shift, she was friendlier than she'd been since Amy Brookman's death. Instead of taking over the computer right away, she planted herself in front of me, too invasive of my space for comfort.

"What's the latest on that woman's murder?" she asked. "The morning paper didn't say much."

I hadn't had time to look at the paper, but I should have known they would carry the story. Despite all the recent drive-by shootings, a murder like this one would be front-page news. And especially since the victim's young daughter had died under mysterious circumstances only three weeks ago.

"I don't know any more than you do," I said.

"Sure you do."

"Why are you so interested, Louise?" It wasn't so long since my last staff pharmacist had turned out to be a killer. For one wild moment, I was afraid Louise had somehow been behind the two murders. Maybe that was why she'd been quick to blame me for Amy's death, but, I admitted, I knew of no connection between Louise and the Brookman family.

"The mother of one of our customers was murdered. Of course, I'm interested."

"I really don't know anything more," I repeated. Her words reminded me that I wanted to check my computer records to see whether any of the other people involved in this case filled their scripts at Food Go.

It would have to wait, I thought. No way was I going to do that in front of Louise. Tomorrow, I'd be on the night shift again. Karen, our technician, would be working, and she could take over the window and phones while I did a computer search.

I got through the rest of my workday, trying not to worry about Jeremy. He hadn't called, but that could mean Lupe never gave him my message.

Just as I was ready to check out, Denise appeared in front of the pharmacy. "Come on," she said, "I'll buy you a late dinner."

"Thanks, Denise, but I really want to get away from the store."

"Do I look like that kind of cheapskate? I mean a real restaurant, not the Food Go coffee shop. We'll go where the presentations are dazzling and the service is by anyone but Denise Seaford."

I laughed for the first time that day. "Not Denny's either?" I asked. When we were both on the same shift, we often went to Denny's or the Village Inn after work.

"Not even Taco Bell."

We both walked into the office and checked out. The parking lot was crowded, but since we were employees, it didn't make any difference. Even on slow days, we had to park toward the back, leaving the close-in spaces for customers.

"Okay, I give up. Where to?"

"I'll tell you what. Leave your car and let's ride together. That way we'll have more time to talk."

"You just don't want to admit we're going to some fast-food place."

We kept up the banter until we were rolling along Scottsdale Road. "The Backstage," she said, naming a popular restaurant on the Scottsdale Mall. Then she turned serious. "Is that okay, Ruthie? I know it's been rough for you, and I thought you needed a cheerful place for dinner."

We found a space a block away from the parklike mall that adjoins Old Town Scottsdale and walked upstairs and through the colorful terrace. The restaurant was buzzing with people, many of them seated at the outdoor tables, but we agreed that an early November evening was cool enough for indoor dining. I looked around at the brightly dressed servers and the chattering crowd and did feel my mood lighten.

"What do you think of Sterling?" Denise suddenly asked as we studied the menu.

"This isn't the right time to ask that question. He got pretty upset with me on the phone this morning." I told her about our conversation.

"He's right, Ruthie. I remember what it was like when Frank Moreway questioned me last summer, insinuating that I had an affair with Harry Stokes."

I knew that Harry Stokes had figured prominently in both of our daydreams before he married Betsy. Although they were customers of mine, I hadn't known Betsy was Michael Loring's daughter. And when I'd seen Michael with her right after Harry's death, I'd been convinced she liked older men and was ready to replace her departed husband with Michael.

Too bad Patricia couldn't possibly be another daughter,

I thought, but I had seen the closeness between her and Michael. This time, I couldn't be mistaken.

"Sterling will be with me tomorrow when I see the police again."

"If you get a chance . . . I mean if it comes up naturally . . . Can you bring me into the conversation?" Denise suddenly seemed transfixed by the menu in front of her, as if she were looking for the one perfect entrée.

"What do you want me to say?"

"You know. Try to find out what he thinks about me."

"Okay, I'll just casually ask when he's going to take you out."

"Ruthie," she said and then realized I was teasing her. She smiled. "Who knows? Maybe the direct approach would work. We're not teenagers, after all."

"I'll try," I promised, "but don't be disappointed."

"I won't."

I knew she really believed she could be casual about his reaction, but I was afraid for her. Sterling Harraday seemed like a decent human being, but I didn't know him well enough to understand whether his occasional pompous air was just a surface mannerism. I hoped it wouldn't keep him from seeing beyond Denise the waitress to Denise the person I knew, the one who was warm and helpful whenever people needed her.

"We have to talk about that young girl," she said, changing the subject. "We can be sure now that I was right—Amy was murdered—and we need to find the motive."

I told her about Nick, that he was responsible for Amy's pregnancy. She was silent for a long time. Meanwhile, the waitress took our orders. It seemed too late in the evening for a full meal, so I ordered a vegetarian sandwich called "The Earthquake" on rye bread with potato salad and cole slaw.

I waited impatiently for the server to leave, curious to hear what Denise would say. She toyed with her water glass as though she were distracting herself from her thoughts.

"Doesn't it seem ironic?" she said finally.

"What do you mean?" I asked, but something told me what Denise was going to say, because I was childless too and sometimes felt the same way. I knew she loved children. Often enough, I'd seen her in the coffee shop, helping to quiet a crying baby or praising the pictures children drew while waiting for their food. She had told me once that her ex-husband never wanted children.

"He always said we should wait to have a family; the time wasn't right." She looked up at me, and I could see the glint of tears in her eyes. "But the time never was right. I think he just didn't like children. I always thought he'd change his mind, but he never did."

Betsy Stokes's problem had been similar, I remembered. Her husband, much older than she was and with grown children from his previous marriage, hadn't wanted a baby either. I wondered how that child, whose father had died during the first months of Betsy's pregnancy, would fare. At least Betsy could easily support her baby emotionally and materially. Denise, on the other hand, had all she could manage to take care of herself. Her dream of going back to school to become a dental technician, the dream that led her to try borrowing money from Harry Stokes and then made her a suspect when he died, seemed perpetually out of reach.

"No one but the people involved can say what was right or wrong," I told her. "You did the best you could at the time."

"I know that," Denise said. "And until all this happened with Amy Brookman, I hardly ever let it into my mind. Now, I think about Amy all the time and how her baby was unwanted even before her miscarriage. Knowing that her mother's boyfriend was the father, I understand why she intended to place her baby with strangers. I want to kill that man with my bare hands."

"Too bad he wasn't the victim instead of Leila, but maybe they'll get him for her murder."

"Much as I hate to say so, Ruthie, I don't believe he did it."

I was surprised. "What do you mean? Surely you don't

think it was Jeremy . . . or me," I finished, just as our sandwiches arrived.

"Of course not. Nick just seems too obvious."

Denise's main fault, it always seems to me, is a tendency to confuse fiction with reality. I tried not to sound as exasperated as I felt. "This isn't a movie. In real life, the most likely person usually *is* the murderer."

"Not always."

"I'll grant you that. Now tell me who you suspect and why."

"Faith Sommers."

"An interesting choice, but don't forget the why," I reminded her.

"Ruthie, you saw her that day. The way she looked. Those people are fanatics."

"But why would she murder Amy?"

"What better way to scare teenagers into abstinence? I tell you it sure would have scared me at the time."

"I'll mention her to Detective Moreway tomorrow. He's in a better position to check on her than we are." Then I remembered Leila. "Why the second murder?" I asked.

"Don't forget, we saw Faith with Amy's aunt that day. It's very possible that she knew both sisters. Maybe Leila found out something that pointed to Faith."

"Denise, I know your dramatic sense zeros in accurately sometimes. But this is too farfetched, even for you."

"We'll see," she said.

"Anyhow other than talking to Frank Moreway, there's nothing we can do."

"We can turn up at her next demonstration. She has them all the time."

I bit into my sandwich and tasted avocado and melted cheese. Denise sat there without eating, obviously waiting for my response. "Aside from everything else, it wouldn't do one bit of good now that she knows us."

"You could say you're interested in promoting teenage abstinence." Her eyes, shadowed in electric blue today to match her blue and white striped dress, opened wide as she tried to convince me.

"Denise, you know I see pregnant teenagers all the time,

but I don't intend to join any demonstrators.''

"I can't think of another way to see more of Faith Sommers.''

By this time, we had both stopped eating. "I understand what you're trying to do," I told Denise. "It's just not something I can carry out.''

"Now that I think of it, you're right. You never could lie convincingly.''

I laughed. "You make that sound like an insult.''

"You're such a straight arrow, Ruthie. In books, the sleuths are always breaking into people's houses or offices. And they lie like crazy when it's for a good cause.''

"Real people don't do that," I said.

"Could be they don't break into places, but you'd be surprised how much lying goes on.'' She shook her head at me. "You deal with the public all day long, same as I do. Don't tell me you haven't been lied to over and over.''

I thought of the times customers tried to get their prescriptions ahead of other people, claiming they had to catch a plane. Or the ones who brought back half-used bottles of pills insisting that I'd miscounted. But those were in the minority. Most of my customers were decent people, wanting only to get well quickly.

"And what about the really nice customers you have at the coffee shop?'' I asked. "Surely you see more good ones.''

"Yes, but at the coffee shop, I'm not involved in life and death situations. You're involved in one, and I think it's okay to fib for a worthy cause.''

"No sense getting into the ends versus the means debate, Denise. People have never been able to agree on that one.''

"Okay, closed subject. I see I can't change your mind.''

I realized she probably would attempt to contact Faith Sommers on her own. Since I was convinced the murderer was Nick and not Faith, I decided not to worry about it.

We paid for our food and left the restaurant, talking about inconsequential things on the way back to the Food Go parking lot to get my car. As we pulled into the lot, I saw Lupe Douglas framed in the entrance lights of the supermarket.

"Stop the car," I yelled to Denise.

She pulled up to the no parking zone in front of the store and we both jumped out. "Lupe," I said. "Where's Jeremy? What's happening?"

"You're the one I came to see," she said. "They arrested Jeremy for murder, and it's all your fault."

Seventeen

We stood there in the parking lot, next to the open doors of Denise's old black Ford, and stared at Lupe. I'd never before seen her look so distraught, not even when her little boy's attention deficit disorder was at its worst.

"Impossible," I said. "No one could really believe Jeremy killed her."

She was rubbing her hands over her cheeks, pulling them down in a grotesque pattern, and I could tell now why her face looked so strange. "Easy to say. You're probably the one who did it."

"Pull yourself together, Lupe. Ruthie would never harm anyone."

"I'm sorry. I don't know what I'm saying anymore."

"Why don't you get in, so we can talk without being overheard?" Denise said and gestured to her car. It was a good suggestion, considering I'd already noticed Food Go customers staring at us as they pushed shopping carts out of the supermarket. I just hoped Lupe wasn't too overwrought to go along with it. But she got right into the front passenger seat, and I reached around to open the back door, getting in so Denise could drive to a more secluded part of the lot.

While she parked the car, I wondered about Jeremy. Aside from the fact that I knew and liked him, I had seen how shocked and miserable he looked when he told me about Leila's death. Unless he was a terrific actor, and I'd never noticed such talent before, I was sure he couldn't have murdered her.

"Tell us what happened," I said to Lupe.

"You already know he handled that dressing table stool. You're probably the one who told the police."

"We've been through that already," I said and then realized I should be more patient with her. "Lupe, I don't for one minute believe Jeremy killed her. And I'll do anything I can to help convince the police." I leaned closer toward the front seat, trying to make her understand I was sincere.

"What can *you* do? Eric can't even get him out on bail."

"We've got a good lawyer . . ." Denise started to say.

What a time to drum up business for Sterling, I thought, and then decided I was being unfair to Denise. She was just trying to help.

"We already have one," Lupe said. "And Eric's a cousin. If anyone will look out for our interests, Eric will." She moved sideways on the front seat and looked back to face me. "I'm sure *you* know that."

I ignored the comment, but the bitterness in her voice unsettled me. She's terrified for Jeremy, I thought. No one can blame her for lashing out at other people.

"Don't you see, Lupe. I'm the main witness . . . the main willing one," I corrected myself, "to say that Jeremy had a reason to handle that chair and did it openly. And Tommy will have to back me up even if Nick won't."

"Tommy has disappeared," she said.

"What?" This opened up an entirely new line of reasoning. "Then why did the police arrest Jeremy? If Tommy ran off, that's surely suspicious."

"His folks say he disappeared before Leila . . ." Her voice broke here, which surprised me because I had the impression she wasn't fond of her sister-in-law.

"I'm sure the police are looking for Tommy," Denise said. "Even if he ran away first, that doesn't let him off the hook."

Lupe calmed down a bit then. We talked a little while longer, and I promised I'd contact her immediately after we saw Detective Moreway the next day. Denise offered to drive her home, but she didn't want to leave the pickup in the lot overnight.

We watched her walk to the truck, get in, and drive away. "She seems to be handling the truck smoothly enough," Denise said. "I'm sure she'll get home okay." She turned back to me. "What a mess, Ruthie. We've got to find the real murderer."

"I don't think we can do it. It's a job for the police."

"You did it before."

"And nearly got killed in the process. Whoever it is— Nick, Faith, Tommy—has killed twice."

"Are you afraid?" Denise asked.

"Of course, I'm afraid. If you think accusing me of fear will change my mind about seeing Faith Sommers, it won't work."

"I'll call you as soon as I find out when she plans to hold her next demonstration," Denise said, and dropped me at my car.

The next morning, I met my attorney as planned at the Scottsdale Police Department. He looked very lawyerly in a navy suit with a fine pinstripe and a red and navy striped power tie. I was sure he'd never wear brown shoes with such a suit and, despite my worry about Jeremy, glanced down to see highly polished black ones. It was probably a foolish generalization, but I decided he'd be a match for Frank Moreway.

We were led to the same office I was interviewed in earlier. The men introduced themselves to each other and we were motioned to seats in front of Frank's desk. As usual, he remained standing, hovering over us.

"Please be seated," Sterling Harraday told him. "I find it hard to crane my neck when I speak to people."

Frank hesitated momentarily. "I certainly wouldn't want you to be uncomfortable, Counselor," he said.

How much more easily Sterling handles Detective Moreway than I do, I thought. I wondered if it was male bonding or Sterling's legal training and experience that made the difference.

"My client insists on making a statement that she hopes will help Jeremy Douglas," Sterling said carefully.

"Fine, but before we get to that, I want to go over one or two things in the statement she made Tuesday night."

"And why wasn't she advised to secure counsel that night?"

"She came here voluntarily, Counselor," Frank Moreway said.

"Hereafter, Mrs. Morris will not be interviewed unless I'm at her side," Sterling told him blandly. "I hope that's understood."

"I don't know what the problem is. We certainly don't suspect her of any crime. As you well know, someone else is under arrest at this point."

"At this point," Sterling said, "but that was not the case Tuesday evening."

Detective Moreway didn't dispute his words, but began going over the same questions he'd asked me that night. He brought up the brass stool several times, and I described how Leila had given Tommy her own chair and remained standing until Jeremy got the dressing table stool for her.

"How did you know it was from a dressing table?" Frank Moreway asked me; it was a new question.

"Any woman would recognize it. You see them all over. This one had brass legs and a pink cushion. It couldn't have been from anything but a dressing table—or I guess some people call them 'vanities' nowadays." I thought for a moment. "Besides, Jeremy told us he was going to the master bedroom to get another chair," I remembered.

"And why did Jeremy get it? Why not the boyfriend, Nick?"

"Jeremy has good manners," I said coldly. "Nick is a brute."

Sterling coughed warningly. "I don't care," I said. "Nick is the one you should be arresting."

The detective ignored my comment. "So Jeremy knew his way around his sister-in-law's bedroom?"

I stared at Frank Moreway. "What are you implying this

time? Back when Harry Stokes died, you tried to prove that either Denise or I or both of us had affairs with him. Don't you know any decent people?''

"Mrs. Morris," Sterling said warningly.

"You're supposed to be on my side," I said to him, and then realized how childish I sounded. "I'm sorry. I guess indignation doesn't do anyone any good."

Detective Moreway smiled for the first time. "Accepted. I'm trying to get an impression of the various people involved and their relationships with each other." He looked through the notes on his desk. "I'll rephrase the question."

"Please do," I said.

"You've already let me know that you believe in Jeremy Douglas. The best way you can help him is to stop trying to protect him. If he's innocent, he doesn't need your protection, and you may be doing more harm than you realize." He stopped and looked intently at me. "You're an intelligent woman. You must have formed some impressions about these people."

"I'll try to fill you in," I said.

"Let's start with Leila's husband. You told me he threatened to get Nick."

"I also said I don't know him well enough to judge whether he meant it. Any father would explode under the circumstances."

"That may be, but we're not guessing about violence here. We have a body."

"Detective Moreway," I said. "We're not getting anywhere. If Nick were the victim, I'd probably suspect Quentin. But what motive did Quentin have to kill Leila?''

"What if he blamed his wife for everything?"

"That's really reaching."

"You'd be surprised what sets people off."

Sterling interrupted here. "This is pointless, Detective. You're wasting my client's time. She came here to give you evidence, not to conjecture."

"On the contrary. I have great respect for Mrs. Morris's insights. Has she told you how she helped us in the past?"

"If that's the case, why did you treat her like a suspect the other night?"

I was surprised to see Frank Moreway look uncomfortable. "Occupational hazard," he told us.

"Maybe it would help if I knew more about the crime," I said, surprising myself.

"You know I can't do that."

"Why not? Reporters always manage to get the details."

"I will tell you this," he said. "The only fingerprints on the chair other than Leila's were Jeremy's. They were on the rim of the seat, which is consistent with the way you say he handled the chair that night. But the murderer held the chair by the legs and wiped all the prints off them. And that's all I'm going to tell you."

"Why weren't any of Nick's prints on the stool? After all, he lived there."

He continued as if he hadn't heard me. "What about the young man, Tommy? How did he act toward Leila?"

"Leila was the one he wanted to talk to."

"But you told me he was waiting to see her alone. Did he blame Leila for her daughter's problems?"

"Problems?" Now I was really annoyed. He was minimizing Amy's seduction and the resultant pregnancy.

I looked at my $145 an hour attorney and then at Frank Moreway. Neither one of them responded. "Tommy was afraid of Nick," I told them. "I think that's the only reason he was trying to see Leila alone.

"Look," I continued, "none of them threatened Leila, and I don't know of any strong motive—unless she found out who exchanged the pills that killed Amy."

"Obviously, that conclusion is to your advantage."

Sterling Harraday interrupted. "We won't discuss that now, Detective. It may be prejudicial to my client if the civil lawsuit materializes."

Frank Moreway allowed his surprise to show, perhaps deliberately. "I can easily ask the girl's father. This is your client's chance to tell her side of the story."

"Go ahead then," Sterling advised me.

"I told you about it the other night, Detective Moreway."

"Let's have all the details this time."

I explained again what had happened. "This second murder makes things very clear," I insisted.

"And gives you an opportunity to exonerate yourself of having made a fatal mistake," Frank Moreway said.

"There was no mistake. That's why we made this appointment in the first place. I wanted to inform you that Nick had every reason to kill Amy. And Leila's murder makes it even more certain."

"Are you trying to tell me you've never made a mistake in filling a prescription?"

"This is beginning to sound like a fishing expedition," Sterling said, rising from his chair. "If you have nothing new to ask my client, I believe it's past time for us to leave."

"She needs to give an official statement about that dressing table stool so we can release Jeremy Douglas," he said.

I was so relieved for Jeremy and Lupe's sakes, I barely heard Sterling caution me to confine my words only to that brass stool. Frank Moreway called someone in to take down my statement. Before he allowed me to sign, Sterling read it over slowly and carefully.

"That's all for now," Detective Moreway told us. "But Ruthie," he said, dropping his more formal manner, "if you think of anything else, I want you to contact me immediately. No more amateur attempts at solving murder."

"Don't worry," I told him. And it was at that precise moment that I decided to check on Faith Sommers, provided Denise would then come with me to talk to Nick.

Eighteen

Sterling Harraday and I walked out of police headquarters into the bright sunlight of Scottsdale in early November. "It's customary," he said, "when you hire someone to represent you, to follow his advice."

His dark eyes were alert behind the horn-rimmed glasses, but his expression was mild. I thought I could detect a smile trying to break through the slight pomposity I was determined to overlook.

"I'm worried about Jeremy," I said.

"That does you credit."

Not his air so much, I decided, but the choice of words made him seem pompous. Although I couldn't believe he and Denise had much in common, I had promised to sound him out. If he went back to his office now, I'd never have the opportunity again. I tried but couldn't find an excuse to detain him.

"We should discuss our strategy," Sterling said.

"Yes."

"My other morning appointment canceled, so I'm free until one o'clock. When do you have to be at the pharmacy?"

"At two."

"Then let's get lunch somewhere," he said. "I promise I won't bill you for the time." There was that flash of humor finally coming through.

"In that case, let lunch be on me."

"Why don't we take both cars so we won't have to

come back here? Shall we go to Jacqueline's?'' he asked, naming a Scottsdale restaurant that specialized in salads, quiches, and delicious baked goods.

Sterling arrived there first. He has that in common with Denise, I thought, as I joined him. They both drive much faster than I do. It was somewhat early for lunch, and the restaurant wasn't too crowded. We requested patio seating and were shown to a brightly covered table amid the greenery, an oasis that effectively screened out the adjacent parking lot. The waitress took our orders—iced tea and a vegetable quiche for me, coffee and a Caesar salad with chicken for Sterling.

I thought of an opening that would provide me with the means to mention Denise and try to discern whether he was at all interested in her. "This is more relaxing for me than the coffee shop at Food Go.''

"I guess you find it convenient to eat there,'' he said.

This was it. "Also, Denise is a good friend. I enjoy talking with her.''

"She seems very concerned for you.''

"Denise is that kind of person,'' I told him. "She always cares about people.'' It was his move, and I waited to hear whether he'd change the subject.

The waitress returned with our beverages. No frilly green Food Go aprons here. I saw that she was an attractive blonde with short, curly hair—much younger than Denise. Sterling didn't seem to notice her at all.

"And you socialize outside of work?''

I felt myself stiffen. If he revealed any hint of snobbery, I was prepared to tell him off. Then I would find another attorney.

"Denise has been divorced for some time. I was widowed about two years ago. She was wonderful when Bob died, and I got to know her better.'' I decided to go further. "It may sound corny to say so, but I think of Denise as one of those rare people who are good through and through. I don't mean that she's perfect,'' I added, thinking how her penchant for melodrama sometimes irritated me, "but I value her immensely as a friend.''

The waitress appeared with our food, and he was silent

for a time. I decided I wasn't going to speak first. If I wanted to discover whether there was a chance for Denise and Sterling to get together, I must hear what he had to say.

My quiche was moist and herbed just right. I ate slowly, waiting, and saw that Sterling also was using his food to postpone further conversation. Funny, I thought, if I were interested in him, I wouldn't be able to keep quiet and wait. But for someone else's sake, I could play the game.

"I'm divorced, too," he said. "More recently than Denise."

"Were you married long?"

"Fifteen years. I have two children, a boy of twelve and a girl of ten." He cut his salad carefully and began eating. "They're with me on weekends."

I wondered if Denise knew he had kids. Perhaps Sterling was using me to transfer information as I attempted to do the same. "That's difficult," I said.

"It's worked out so far." He stopped as if wondering how much to tell me. "She remarried almost at once."

That seemed to be a coded message, a way to let me know that the divorce hadn't been his idea. "But you haven't remarried," I said, more as a statement than a question. Since I was probably about ten years older than he, I figured I could probe without any possibility of my motives being misunderstood.

"No," he said. "I've been afraid of the rebound effect."

This surely was meant to be passed along to Denise. I could think of no other reason for his confidences. I cut into the crust of my quiche, the part I liked best. Sterling also had started to eat more steadily, and neither of us spoke.

After a while, he changed the subject and asked why I was so sure of Jeremy's innocence. "Even if his fingerprints on the stool can be explained, that doesn't preclude later prints that he wiped off."

"Yes. And he certainly knew where to find it if he wanted to use it as a weapon." I put down my fork and met Sterling's reflective gaze. "But he doesn't have a motive," I said.

"You mean, he doesn't have one we know about."

"Look," I explained patiently. "Jeremy has a wife and son he treasures. Why would he kill his niece and sister-in-law?"

"How well do you know him?"

"Mostly from Food Go."

"And you think that's enough to judge how he'd act under pressure? Do you see him socially?"

"What are you driving at?"

"I'm merely trying to understand the situation," he answered blandly.

"And I'm good at catching nuances," I said. "You're hinting at some sort of relationship. Even Frank Moreway didn't go that far this time."

"This time?"

I found I had to tell Sterling about Harry Stokes's death and the detective's suspicion that I'd had an affair with Harry. "Of course, he was completely wrong," I finished. "But Harry was older than I am; you surely know that Jeremy is much younger."

"Experience has taught me to disregard age when I'm trying to understand motivation," he said. "All right, I admit I wanted to see your reaction. If I'm representing you, I need to be sure I know why you haven't kept me informed or followed my advice."

We'd come full circle. "It's precisely because I have nothing to hide," I said and ignored him while I stopped a passing server for an iced tea refill.

"How does Jeremy get along with the rest of the family? I understand Leila's husband is only his half-brother."

"There's no 'only' to it," I said. "He refers to Quentin as his brother."

"You didn't answer my question."

I thought about what I'd learned, that the family hadn't accepted Lupe because of her Hispanic heritage. Surely Jeremy had indicated that was in the past. "They seemed fairly close," I told him. "Amy babysat for their little boy."

As soon as the words were out, I regretted them. Maybe it was better not to emphasize that particular closeness.

"And I understand they wanted to adopt her baby," Sterling said.

Who could have told him that, I wondered. Surely not Denise. "I don't see what that has to do with anything."

"On the contrary," he said. "I can come up with some interesting motives. It wouldn't be the first time someone killed because the other person thwarted his wishes."

"You're really reaching now. Maybe if Lupe and Jeremy were childless and this was their only chance at adoption, but . . ."

"I've thought this over carefully," Sterling said. "There's a very good possibility that the wrongful death suit will be dropped if we can link the two deaths. Or, worst case, we go to court and I raise enough doubts because of Leila's murder to win the suit." He stopped as the waitress returned to clear our plates.

"Some dessert today?" she asked.

Sterling looked inquiringly at me. I shook my head. "We'll pass," he said, "but we'd like more coffee and iced tea, please."

"You don't understand," I told him. "Naturally, if we have to go to court, I prefer to win. But even if we win, it will ruin me professionally."

"Then, we must get serious about this. You can't afford sentimental objections to pinpointing Jeremy—or anyone else, for that matter."

"I wasn't being sentimental," I told him. "But surely you can see that Nick Kenmore is a much more likely suspect."

"Or the young man who disappeared. The police are looking at both of them. Meanwhile, you've been trying to clear a viable candidate."

"So, you're telling me I should have let Jeremy stay in jail. Don't you realize how distraught his wife was?"

"And that's exactly my point about sentimentality."

Our beverages were refilled and the waitress, obviously well trained, put the check midway between Sterling and me. I picked it up.

''What I'm saying,'' my lawyer told me, ''is that Detective Moreway is right. The police don't need amateurs muddying the waters.''

Sterling was the second person this morning to try and keep me from doing what I knew I must do. I took my wallet out of my handbag and extracted a credit card, making the process last as long as possible, afraid that if my lawyer looked closely at my face, he would guess my resolve to do exactly the opposite of what he'd just advised. Although I was paying this man $145 an hour for his counsel, I knew I couldn't sit back and wait. I must prove I had not been professionally negligent.

Nineteen

I was sure Tommy's disappearance rather than my evidence about the fingerprints led to Jeremy's release from jail, but I didn't say that to him or to Lupe when I dropped in on them after work that evening. Both of them thanked me for going to the police to support Jeremy's story about the prints.

If anything, Lupe seemed more haggard than she had the night before. Her eyes were red-rimmed, but she was neatly dressed in a flowered housecoat. They kept looking at each other and smiling, and I was ashamed of thinking even for a moment that Jeremy had been infatuated with his sister-in-law.

Lupe insisted on making coffee, but I told her I couldn't stay. "I have to open up tomorrow, and I know you're both early risers, too."

"Thanks for coming by to see how things are," Jeremy said.

Now I felt worse. "Actually, I had another reason. Denise and I want to check out some things about Nick and about that woman who tried to make an example of Amy."

"I'll go with you," Jeremy said.

"No, we won't discover anything that way. But I need you to figure out some plausible excuse to meet with Nick. He knows me, of course, so I can't pretend to be anyone else, even if I wanted to. But there must be some way."

Lupe was always the practical one. "What will you accomplish?"

''I certainly don't expect him to confess to us. I just want to shake him up.''

''That's not very smart if you think he's a murderer,'' Lupe said.

''The police aren't doing anything about Nick. I can't bear to see him get away with murder and besides, I still have to prove I didn't give Amy the wrong pills.''

Jeremy grinned. ''So, if anything happens to my favorite pharmacist, we'll know it was Nick.''

''Or Faith-whatever-her-name,'' Lupe said.

This was small consolation although certainly better than keeping knowledge about my plans from everyone. Since I wasn't foolhardy enough to see Faith or Nick alone, though, I had no reason to be afraid.

''You could tell Nick you need to talk to him about the lawsuit,'' Lupe suggested. ''It sounds plausible to want to know if it's still on.''

''But if I call him, he'll just say a few words on the telephone, and that will be the end of it. I won't get to sound him out.''

''You really expect to trip him up, to somehow make him confess to you?''

I could hear Jeremy's skepticism as he voiced the question. He was forcing me to realize how naive my approach was. ''No,'' I said slowly. ''But even Detective Moreway wanted my impressions of the people involved. I need to be clearer in my mind about them. Right now, I keep thinking I should know what happened, but I can't quite get at it.''

''If you're serious about talking to Nick, just go over there unexpectedly again.''

''I can't watch the house the way Tommy did on the off-chance of catching him at home.''

''The funeral . . .'' Jeremy's voice broke and he started again. ''The funeral is Friday. After that Nick'll probably go back to work. I know I will.'' He fingered his reddish beard, which looked rather scruffy tonight. ''What's your schedule this weekend?''

''Off Saturday, on Sunday.''

''Okay, he works half days on weekends. If you and

Denise get over there Saturday after two o'clock or so, I think you'll find him home.''

"Thanks, Jeremy."

"If that doesn't work, let me know and I'll run interference for you. I can call and act like I need to see him. Then once I have his schedule . . .'' His voice trailed off, and he looked so exhausted that I said my goodbyes and hastily left.

I was afraid Denise would be working on Saturday. Impatient though I was to talk to Nick, I would not go alone. For once, however, our schedules did coincide.

"We should really go to Leila's funeral and observe all of them," she said.

"No way. We have no reason to be there. I only met Leila once, and you never met her at all.''

"So what? Lots of people go to funerals after a sensational murder.''

"Denise, this was only sensational for the family. Otherwise, it's just another crime that people read about in the newspapers—and a fairly ordinary one at that.''

"I'll bet the police will be observing everyone.''

"All the more reason for us to stay away.''

When she realized I wouldn't change my mind about the funeral, Denise said she'd pick me up just before two o'clock on Saturday to try and see Nick, but this wasn't until I told her I agreed we should meet with Faith Sommers again, too.

Meanwhile, I made time to check the Food Go computers but could find none of the names I was looking for. And early Saturday morning, Michael called again from Tucson to tell me he hadn't found any other Coumadin leads either. "You realize it could be someone we haven't even heard of.''

"No," I said. "Jeremy told me he checked it out. At first, the family wasn't supposed to know about the miscarriage. But Amy didn't seem to be doing well, and her aunt decided to call Leila. That night and the next day, all of them were at Virginia's house at one time or another.''

"Then, I'll keep trying. I don't always get people I

know or people who'll talk, so it takes quite a few calls
to each chain of pharmacies. And the independently owned
pharmacies are another problem. Luckily for our purpose,
there aren't too many of those left.''

I thought of my father and what his reaction would have
been to Michael's casual disposal of the former backbone
of the profession. Even though I now worked for the
chains my Dad had hated, I could still be saddened that so
few individually owned drugstores had survived.

Michael didn't mention Patricia and, unwilling to hurt
myself further, neither did I. I didn't tell him about the
plans Denise and I had made. No one was going to talk
me out of doing whatever I could to get at the truth.

After we said goodbye, I stepped outside to check the
weather. It was overcast, which in November meant a
chilly day by Scottsdale standards. I decided to dress casually in my turquoise jogset and a short-sleeved blouse in
a deeper shade of turquoise. If the sun did come out later,
I could always take off the jacket to the jogset and still be
comfortable.

I was determined not to be nervous about the meeting
with Nick, but I found it hard to stay calm. Usually, I tried
to avoid working around the house on Saturday. Even
though so many years had passed, and I was no longer an
observant Jew in most respects, those early restrictions
were hard to relinquish. Not for the first time, I thought
how ironic that I had given up Michael for reasons that
turned out to be transitory. Well, it was too late now.

Denise arrived on time, and I directed her to the house
where Leila had lived with Nick. I assumed he hadn't
moved since Jeremy would have let me know about any
change.

We planned our strategy.

"I guess I'll do the talking," I said, more nervous than
I cared to admit at the prospect.

"And I'll flirt with him."

I looked at Denise. She also wore a jogset, but hers was
black and, despite the cooler weather, I could see she had
on a bandeau top. Even wearing the jacket, she exposed a

great deal of tanned flesh. "Are you serious? I told you, he's a brute."

"Could be. But he's surely not going to attack me. I just thought it would be a good idea to try and get him interested. Maybe meet with him later on and see what I can find out."

I looked dubious. Despite her lovely gray eyes and slim figure, Denise didn't interest men that easily.

"Ruthie, I know what you're thinking. But I never have trouble attracting the wrong ones. It's only the guys like Sterling that I can't seem to make any progress with."

That reminded me I had talked about Denise to him and had gathered some information about his personal life. I told Denise what I'd learned. "Do you really like him that much?" She nodded, so I asked, "Why?"

"Probably because he doesn't come on to me. You have no idea what it's like working as a waitress. Some men seem to think that makes you fair game."

She rarely complained, and I kicked myself for not realizing how unpleasant some of her customers must be. Her job made mine seem wonderful, even though I sometimes had to placate angry patients. And many of mine are there because they're not feeling well, I told myself. Or they may be in pain. You'd think people would be in a better mood when they drop in for a snack at the coffee shop.

I nearly didn't recognize the house. Even though it had been dark when Jeremy and I were there, I had an impression of a modest but well-kept home. Today, I saw that much of the Bermuda grass had died, but no one had planted a winter lawn. What was left of the summer lawn looked like it hadn't been mowed recently. Leila had struck me as house-proud, and I couldn't believe that so much had changed in so short a time.

"Where should I park?" Denise whispered, as if someone could overhear her.

I found myself whispering back. "Go up a few houses. Over there. By that palm tree. He won't be able to see the car from his windows."

"Was that his van in the driveway?"

"I don't know. Let's just go up and ring the doorbell." Anything was better than sitting in the car, worrying what I would say and how Nick would react.

The same harsh voice I remembered repeated the words I'd heard that other night. "If you're selling something, we don't want any."

I wondered about the "we." Maybe it was habit.

Denise pushed the doorbell again, and this time Nick Kenmore opened the door. "What do you want?" he said.

All the carefully rehearsed excuses fled my mind, and I found myself gaping at him, unable to say a word. He stared back at me but didn't shut the door in our faces as I half expected him to do.

"May we come in?" Denise asked politely. "We want to talk."

Again I anticipated rejection, but he held open the door and waved us in. "You interrupted my lunch," he said. "You got something to say, talk while I eat. Maybe I'll listen."

We followed him into the kitchen. I looked around, expecting to find dirty dishes piled up everywhere, but it was surprisingly neat. Nick took a seat at the far end of the table, which was set with an oval placemat. I could see one half-eaten sandwich and a mound of potato chips. No plate, which explained the clean countertops. Without waiting for an invitation, we pulled out chairs and sat down, too.

"Okay, what can I do for you girls?"

I winced, but my prepared script suddenly came back to help me. "First, of course, we want to tell you how sorry we are about Leila. I only met her that one time, but she was decent to me despite everything."

"Despite everything," he echoed. "Why don't you come out and say what you mean?"

"I was planning to."

He picked up a handful of chips and crunched on them. "You want to know if I'm still gonna sue the pants off you."

Again I winced, wondering how Amy had let this insensitive man sweet talk her into a relationship, however briefly. I guessed a psychologist would have found a rivalry issue with her mother or something along those lines.

"Yes, my friend does want to know your plans," Denise said.

"And Jeremy thinks you're so smart," Nick said to me. "Don't you know only the lawyers are supposed to talk to each other? I bet yours don't know you're here today."

I suddenly felt chilled. Was this a clever way to find out if anyone was aware of our visit to Nick's place? Don't be foolish, I told myself. Even a double murderer would hesitate to kill two more people when anyone might know we'd been to see him.

"Lupe and Jeremy know where we are."

He laughed and took a bite of his sandwich. "If you're afraid of me, why didn't you just use the telephone? Why pop in here?"

We were prepared for that question. "It's easier to discuss something like this in person."

"So discuss. I'm listening."

Denise and I looked at each other. "You never did answer the question," she said.

"And I ain't about to."

"Does that mean you haven't decided?"

"It means whatever you want it to mean. I suppose your shyster told you we offered to settle. Take it. You'll never get a better deal."

If I wanted to see his reactions, I would have to be direct. "I don't believe you have any possibility of a lawsuit anymore."

"Lady, anyone can sue anyone else. It's the American way." He scarfed more potato chips and got up to refill his supply from a bag on the countertop.

"Don't try to tell us that Leila's murder had nothing to do with Amy's death. Both of them were murdered, and you know it."

He slammed his fist on the table, and I forced myself not to react. This man was used to bullying people, and I didn't intend to let him frighten me the way he had the last time I had encountered him. I continued, keeping my voice even. "When we find out who killed her mother, we'll know who killed Amy."

"If you're trying to pin it on me, you just cleared me. I can prove I was at work when Leila . . . when it happened." For the first time, his voice showed emotion, and I began to see that he might really have cared for Leila.

"Yes, but I happen to know you have the kind of job where you can take off and ride around during the day, testing the cars you repair."

"Sounds like you been getting an earful from Jeremy. Remember, he's the one they arrested—not me."

"And they released him right away. If you're so innocent, why didn't you tell them how Jeremy's fingerprints got on that chair."

"Why should I?"

I was horrified to see Denise remove the jacket to her jogging suit. Not now, I thought. You're only going to distract him.

He was staring at her and suddenly got up. The abrupt movement startled me. I found myself perspiring with suppressed anxiety but kept my own jacket on. He walked over to the refrigerator, took out some cans of soft drink, and handed one to each of us. "This house is always too warm," he said.

It was such an ordinary gesture and such a considerate one, it was hard to sustain my image of him as villain. I pulled the tab on the can and slowly sipped the cola. At least it gave me time to think. This visit wasn't going to accomplish anything unless I confronted him directly.

"You say you have an alibi," I told him. "But alibis don't always mean anything. You had motives to kill both of them, and I told the police all about you."

I expected a violent reaction, but he laughed. "You're such a busybody!"

My face felt flushed. He was right in a way, but I had every reason to try and prove Amy had been murdered. And right now, it seemed the best way to do that was to discover what really happened to Leila.

"Did you also tell the police about that kid's motive? Don't you think it's strange that he ran away?"

"What motive?" Denise asked.

"Your friend here is so busy trying to pin something on me that she believed every word he said," Nick answered her. He stared at each of us in turn, his face sullen and angry at the same time. "I don't know why I bother to talk to you."

"If you think Tommy's the murderer, then don't stop now. Give us your reasons."

"And . . ." he taunted.

"And we may believe you." Denise said.

"So what. Why should I care what you girls think?"

"You deal with the public in your job. Suspicion isn't good for you," Denise told him.

"Are you threatening me?"

"No," I hurried to say. "We're just trying to get to the bottom of this."

"In that case, talk to Amy's father. He came around here after Leila's funeral, threatening to beat me up." Nick stopped to finish the remains of his sandwich. "I'd like to see him try. A guy who couldn't even hold onto his wife."

"All very macho," I said surprising myself, "but you still haven't told us anything concrete."

"You want concrete. Here's concrete—back when Amy lived at her father's place, Quentin had to get a restraining order to keep that kid away from his daughter." He looked pleased with himself when he saw our startled expressions.

"I don't believe you. That young man loved her."

"That young man," he said, his voice mimicking me, "is a con artist."

Twenty

"**D**on't think we won't check this out," I said, although I was beginning to wonder about Tommy despite my earlier convictions. His disappearance, coupled with this new information, certainly seemed suspicious. If only I could discover whether he also had access to Coumadin. I decided to redouble my efforts at locating the pharmacy his parents patronized.

Even though there seemed to be no point trying to find out more from Nick, I made a last effort. "You're trying to implicate Tommy, but we know you're the one who had access to Coumadin."

"Lady," he said, his voice serious rather than taunting this time, "before Amy died, I never even heard of that drug."

"You expect us to believe you lived here with Leila and didn't know she was on Coumadin."

"I don't expect you to believe nothing."

"So why are you claiming you didn't know about the blood thinner?" Denise asked.

"Leila once said there was heart disease in her family. I knew she took something to head off that kind of trouble, but we never talked about details." He stood now and loomed over us, a stance that would have seemed menacing on anyone's part but was more threatening coming from Nick.

"I got better things to do than waste time with you

girls,'' he said and led us through the house to the front door.

There didn't seem to be any reason to avoid following him, so we left. Back in Denise's car, we discussed the visit. "What do you think?" Denise asked. "Are you still convinced he's the one?"

"I'm more confused than before," I admitted. "Do you see him as a murderer?"

"Could be."

"On the positive side, the police probably didn't check his alibi that thoroughly once they arrested Jeremy. And now they have Tommy to look for." I leaned back against the headrest and closed my eyes. "Also, despite his claims to the contrary, we know Nick had access to Coumadin. It still makes sense to figure Leila realized what happened once she saw he had a motive to kill her daughter and access, through her, to the drug that did it. Maybe she even noticed some of her medication was missing and that tipped her off."

"How do we prove it?"

"We can't. But I can keep hounding Frank Moreway so that he has to investigate Nick more carefully. The trouble is I'm not sure anymore." I opened my eyes again and turned toward Denise. "Did you get the impression he really cared for Leila despite everything?"

"Hard to believe, but it could be."

"And he didn't act like a guilty person."

"How does a guilty person act? No one realized who killed Harry Stokes until it was nearly too late," she reminded me. "Let's go to see Faith now." She inserted the ignition key and started her car, gunning the motor in her haste to interview our next suspect.

I had expected someone in the public eye to have an unlisted number but, surprisingly, we had found Faith Sommers in the phone book. She lived in North Scottsdale in one of the newer areas, marked by houses with terracotta tile roofs in contrast to the ubiquitous red tile of the older neighborhoods. Again, we took the chance of finding our quarry at home. We didn't dare risk refusal by telephoning for an appointment.

The streets curved in disorienting circles, some of which led to dead ends. Denise, who was more confident in her driving and her sense of direction than I, continued searching, unflustered. Despite the richness of the homes, the area seemed barren to me. Even the desert vegetation failed to disguise its newness. Many of the owners had planted citrus and palms, but they were small compared to the full-grown trees I was accustomed to seeing in my older Scottsdale neighborhood. In keeping with the desert look and the need to conserve water, no one had planted lawns.

After losing our way a few times, we found the house. It looked just like all the other homes we had passed, the front dominated by a three-car garage, but the landscaping was more distinctive here. Someone had planted yellow flowers that I couldn't identify around the cactus and decorative rock groupings. And the front walks were bordered with yellow thevetia bushes.

Since the area was so new, I thought for a moment of passing ourselves off as neighbors but couldn't bring myself to lie about it. We walked up to the front door, rang the bell, and waited to be observed through etched glass panels.

Chimes announced our presence, and Faith Sommers herself answered the doorbell. Today, she also wore a jogging outfit, which was standard for Arizona in November, but hers was a dark green silk set. She smiled at us, and I saw no sign of recognition.

"Won't you step in?" she said graciously.

I was surprised. When I was growing up in Tucson, this was exactly the way we responded to people on our doorstep. We would've been considered very rude to react in any other way. Nowadays, though, most people had long since become wary of strangers. We usually found out their business before opening the door and inviting them in.

Denise and I followed her through a large entryway and down two steps into a living room, furnished like some of the upscale model homes I'd seen in magazine ads. Carpets, drapes, and furniture were all off-white. Color in the room came from flowered cornices over the expanse of windows and matching throw pillows on the white sofas and chairs. Through the windows, I could see a rectangular swimming pool like mine, but this one had rock gardens on three sides, giving it a lagoonlike appearance.

"What a lovely pool," I said spontaneously and with absolute sincerity. Swimming pools were no novelty in Scottsdale. Our long, hot summers made them a necessity and even relatively inexpensive homes were built with in-ground pools, but this one was obviously custom-designed.

"Thank you. We enjoy it." She seated us on one white sofa and, poised and waiting to hear our business, sat on an identical one at right angles to us.

When we'd planned this visit, Denise and I had discussed telling Faith we wanted to join her family values group. I couldn't bring myself to lie, however, no matter how important our purpose.

"Do you remember us?" Denise asked.

She looked closely at both of us. "I hope you'll excuse me. My memory for faces has never been very good."

"We were at that demonstration about ten days ago."

She seemed pleased. "You're interested in our movement."

I was tempted to agree but didn't. "If you'll bear with us, Mrs. Sommers, we want to talk about Leila Brookman."

"Sorry, I don't think I know anyone named Leila."

I had been watching closely to see her reaction but could detect no evidence of guile. Even Denise had to see that this woman wasn't implicated in Leila's murder, I decided. Unless Faith had been on the stage, I couldn't believe she knew what we were talking about.

"Surely you remember that last name," Denise said. "Brookman. The girl who died after a miscarriage."

"Oh yes. Amy Brookman. Such a tragedy, and one that should have been avoided."

"It certainly should have been avoided," I agreed. "She was deliberately murdered."

This time, Faith lost some of her poise and gave a slight gasp. I tried to assess whether her reaction was too theatrical to be real but concluded it wasn't overdone. In fact, it sounded quite normal to me.

"I haven't come across anything about that on the news."

"It's only a matter of time," I said.

"Now that her mother's also been murdered," Denise added.

"Are you saying that this Leila was the girl's mother and that she's dead, too?"

"Murdered. You must have seen *that* on TV." Denise's words were so sharp that I realized her suspicions remained alive.

"I never connected the two deaths. Surely it's a coincidence."

"Very unlikely, don't you think?"

"I don't know what to believe." She collected herself. "But why are you here?

This was the moment of truth. We couldn't say we suspected her, but we had to find out if she was involved. I decided the only way to handle this interview was to say exactly what I wanted to know and why.

"Let me tell you what we think happened," I said. "I'm a pharmacist. You probably heard that her family believes I gave Amy the wrong drug."

"I remember now. Virginia Rowland said you did it deliberately, but she seemed overwrought from the tragedy, so I put it out of my mind."

"Virginia was right in saying it couldn't have happened by accident. But I'm not the one who made the substitution. You heard Amy's aunt say she was supposed to take a prescribed drug to prevent excessive bleeding. Instead, she took a blood thinner called Coumadin." I paused and asked one of the crucial questions. "Are you familiar with Coumadin?"

"As a matter of fact, my husband is on that medication."

Denise and I looked at each other. Faith was quick to catch and interpret our reaction. "Surely you're not accusing me," she said.

"I'm not accusing anyone," I told her.

"Then why are you here?"

This was it. She might throw us out, very politely of course, or she might help willingly. And we would have to interpret her reaction, for either course could hide guilt.

"As far as we know, the police don't believe Amy was murdered. Even now, when there's no doubt someone killed her mother, the detective I talked with doesn't seem to connect the two deaths."

"And you have a decided interest in making that connection."

"Well, yes, I do."

"I agree that it does seem rather a coincidence. You still haven't told me why you're here if you don't suspect me of somehow . . ." Her voice trailed off as if the idea was too ridiculous to be voiced.

"We need to talk to everyone who might have information. Then, maybe we can piece it all together."

"I think you've been reading too many mysteries." She smiled to take the sting out of her words, and I was surprised to find that I rather liked Faith Sommers. Despite some negative experiences in a profession that few women entered in my day, I had never been a political activist. And I guess I stereotyped women like Faith as fanatics.

"Did you ever meet Amy?" Denise asked.

"Yes, I met her," Faith said slowly. "I could deny it, but I have nothing to hide. If there's any possibility she was deliberately murdered, then I, too, want that person to be caught."

"Could you tell us the details of your meeting?"

"Her Aunt Virginia brought her to see me."

"Here?"

She nodded. "At the time, Amy was talking about an abortion. Virginia wanted me to show her some of the pictures we have, to talk her out of going through with it."

"Could you tell us exactly what happened?"

"I don't see how that visit could have anything to do with her death, even if it turns out she really was murdered."

"Please," I said. "At this stage, we don't know what's

important. We're trying to learn everything we can about Amy and the people who knew her.''

I waited, uncertain again as to Faith's reaction. She seemed doubtful, too, pausing for a long time. I could see Denise restlessly crossing and uncrossing her legs, and I knew she also was worried.

''Let me think,'' Faith said. ''Amy sat right where you are, and her aunt was over here next to me. I always prefer this sofa because it's closer to the kitchen if I want to bring out any refreshments.''

She looked rather embarrassed for a moment but made no move to offer anything to us. How different from Leila, I thought, with a pang. Leila, whose modest home had probably cost far less than this one, hadn't hesitated to offer hospitality to her unwelcome guests.

Faith continued. ''The girl looked much younger than her age, and she was very quiet. Virginia and I did all the talking.''

''Had you known Virginia before?''

''We met once or twice. She supports our movement.''

''What did Virginia say to you?''

''She called first to make an appointment.'' Faith looked pointedly at us. ''So I knew why they had come. Virginia told me the girl was adamant, which made me decide to approach things carefully.''

''Did she tell you why Amy wanted an abortion?''

''That was what I was supposed to find out.''

''Weren't you surprised she was with her aunt instead of her mother?'' I asked.

''I already knew the mother was a flighty type, not to speak ill of the dead, of course. The girl was living with her aunt, couldn't get along with the mother's boyfriend, I gathered.'' She pursed her lips and turned back into the stereotype I'd originally expected her to be.

''Then Virginia didn't know that her sister's boyfriend was the baby's father.'' I made it a statement, not a question.

Faith gasped once more. ''Some families are so dysfunctional today. I don't know how we're going to cope with their children.''

"Maybe that's why Amy wanted an abortion," Denise said drily. I gave her a look that was meant as a reminder not to antagonize Faith.

"There are other alternatives."

"And did you discuss those with Amy?"

"Of course. That was the point. I understood another aunt was willing to adopt the baby."

So, Lupe's offer to adopt was known before the fact. I had wondered if she and Jeremy had really committed themselves or simply said so after Amy's death. Faith continued without waiting for my questions to prompt her.

"She was such a pathetic girl, so thin, so unhappy. Now that you've told me about the baby's father, I can understand why she seemed so sad. At the time, I thought she was unhappy about her decision. I was sure I could change her mind." Faith's hands were clasped as if in prayer.

"When I showed her the pictures, she started to cry, but we couldn't make her change her mind. Her aunt put her arms around Amy and tried to console her."

I couldn't picture that unyielding woman consoling her niece, but it wasn't the first time I'd misjudged people. And her aunt was the one who took her in, no questions asked, for she obviously had never learned about Nick.

"Sometimes, after I talk to them, they think things over and keep the babies. Or give them up for adoption," Faith said. "I prayed Amy would do that, but then the poor thing miscarried."

"Was Virginia upset?" I asked. Maybe she's the one, I suddenly thought. She had seemed so supportive of her niece, I'd never suspected her before.

"Of course, she was upset. Who wouldn't be?"

"That's not what I meant. Not upset in general, but upset with Amy."

Faith's glance at me seemed contemptuous, and I flinched inwardly, but I told myself I couldn't afford to eliminate anyone from my list of suspects. She was quiet for a few moments, and again I worried that she would freeze us out.

"If you had seen the two of them together, you'd bite your tongue before accusing Virginia."

"I did see the two of them together," I told her, hearing the stiffness in my tone and knowing it was because I was thoroughly ashamed of myself. We'd come here because Denise had pegged this woman as a murderer, and now I was mentally condemning another woman. And I hadn't even given that one a chance to speak for herself as we had with Nick and now were doing with Faith.

"Virginia has a very responsible position. She's administrative assistant to an executive at an electronics company in Tempe. Since she never married or had children of her own, she told me Amy was like a daughter to her."

I remembered my first impression—that they were mother and daughter. But I wasn't naive enough to cross Virginia Rowland off my list for that reason, especially since she did have opportunity, and I didn't know who else besides Nick had the chance to substitute the pills. On the other hand, I could think of no motive for her to kill Amy and even less of a reason for her to murder Leila. For that matter, Denise's suspicion of Faith, resulting from the latter's attempt to use the death politically, seemed rather farfetched to me as I sat in Faith's attractive home. By stretching our imaginations, we could possibly find motives for people like Lupe, Jeremy, and Quentin. I was becoming convinced, however, that only Nick and Tommy had substantial reasons to get rid of both victims.

Faith seemed to be waiting for me to say something, so I obliged. "And that was the last time you saw Amy?"

I observed two spots of red suddenly appear on Faith's high cheekbones, and I began to think I'd dismissed her from my list of suspects too soon. She seemed reluctant to speak.

"You did see her again?"

"Yes." The word was spoken so softly I nearly missed it. "I was at Virginia's that night. She called me."

"I understand why Virginia brought Amy to see you beforehand, but why would she call you to come over after the miscarriage?" I asked.

Faith really appeared flustered now. Finally she sighed and continued. "I know how this is going to sound to both of you in the light of what happened to Amy. Hindsight is a wonderful luxury.''

We waited. She got up and stood looking out through the wall of windows, her back to us. I saw now that french doors were set into that glass wall, their panes matching the window panes. She turned around and faced us again, looking so miserable that for one wild moment, I expected a confession.

''I went there to take pictures.''

''Pictures?''

''You have to understand how much it means to me to convince these young women to remain abstinent.'' She paused. ''Amy seemed so frail when I met her. I knew she'd look a lot worse after the miscarriage.'' Faith's poise had deserted her, and she gazed almost pleadingly at Denise and me.

Suddenly, I understood and I was furious. ''You planned to use Amy's photograph to frighten people. How could you invade her privacy that way? I suppose you also took pictures of her in her coffin,'' I finished.

''One person's privacy isn't as important as countless ruined lives.''

''We've heard that line before,'' Denise said.

''You don't understand . . .''

''I understand only too well,'' Denise told her.

Faith Sommers had collected herself by now and was calm again. ''It's done. We'll have to agree to differ. Just remember that I had her aunt's permission.''

''And what about Amy's consent?''

''Amy was in no position to consent. She didn't seem aware of much that was going on at the time.''

To my way of thinking, that made it worse, but I could see no point in arguing with Faith. She had convinced herself that she was right, and nothing I said would change her mind.

It was Denise who caught something I'd missed. ''What did you mean about things going on at the time? Was anyone else there?''

''Virginia's house was crowded with people.''

Here it was at last. Until now, since I couldn't question

everyone about their whereabouts the way the police could, I'd been limited to looking at motives. Faith Sommers, however, was about to reveal who had the opportunity to switch medications that night. And the more I considered it, the clearer it was to me that the change had to be made the first evening. Once Amy began taking the real Methergine, she couldn't have missed the differences in shade of purple and in shape between that drug and Coumadin, the blood thinner.

''Who else was there?'' I asked, trying to keep the excitement from my voice, afraid she'd refuse to discuss it further.

''Let's see now. I told you I don't have a good memory for people.'' She seated herself again and appeared lost in thought.

My suspicions of her were reawakened, and I wondered if she'd try to implicate other people to dilute the impact of her own visit on our suspicions. I debated whether I should try to prompt her by asking about individuals connected to Amy.

''I didn't see everyone. The father was just leaving as I arrived. And I guess I did meet the mother after all. She was with another man—must have been the one you mentioned, the one who lives with her.''

I waited, nodding slightly at Denise to keep her from interrupting, afraid we'd lose this source of information. Already, I could see how difficult it would be to pinpoint the murderer if so many people had been to see Amy that night.

''There was a boy about Amy's age. I remember thinking he was her brother, but the way he spoke to her, I thought he . . . you know,'' she finished delicately. ''I could see he was in love with her.

''Then, just as I was leaving, two more people came in. I'm not sure I caught the relationship,'' she said almost apologetically. ''I didn't stay long enough to talk to them.''

''What did they look like?''

''My dear, I'm hopeless at that sort of thing. I meet so many people when I speak and when we demonstrate . . .''

They could have been neighbors, friends, anyone. I thought about all the people I'd already met who were involved with Amy. This was going to be a lot more difficult to figure out than Harry Stokes's murder. And I certainly didn't want to put myself or anyone else in danger this time.

"Were they men or women?" Denise prompted. "Young or old?"

"Let's see now. A big man. Oh, yes, the woman was Mexican."

"Hispanic," I corrected automatically.

"Amy's aunt and uncle," Denise said.

"Maybe. I just don't remember."

But to me it seemed indisputable, and I was surprised neither Lupe nor Jeremy had mentioned they'd seen Amy the night of her miscarriage. I wondered what else they were hiding. Perhaps, because I liked him so much, I'd been too quick to explain away Jeremy's fingerprints on the brass stool.

Twenty-one

We thanked Faith Sommers and she graciously told us she was happy to help, but I could see how eagerly she waited for us to go. She had, however, given us important information that we might never have learned elsewhere. Now I had to figure out who was implicated by Faith's story.

Denise was quiet as we left the house and got into her car. To avoid interrupting her thoughts, I waited to speak until I couldn't stand the silence.

"Do you still think Faith is the one?"

"Could be. But I have to admit I'm confused. Tell you what, Ruthie, let's go back to my house and talk it out."

I remembered the last time I'd been to Denise's, the day of the demonstration. That was when I'd first seen Michael and Patricia together. My automatic impulse was to avoid Denise's house now, since she lived next door to Michael's daughter, but I decided the chances of anyone noticing our arrival were slim. Besides, I'd heard nothing from either of them all week, which probably meant they had no new information.

"Good idea," I said. "We do need to sort out our impressions. I keep thinking I'm overlooking something important."

Twenty minutes later when we pulled into Denise's driveway, I tried to be inconspicuous as I scanned the other driveway. No one was in sight.

The air was heavy with the unpleasant odor that per-

meates Scottsdale every autumn when people put in their
winter lawns, overseeding with rye grass. The problem
isn't the grass itself but the animal fertilizer, which is used
to hasten germination. Winter lawns do best here after
nighttime temperatures fall below 60 degrees, which is
usually late September or early October. Since some home-
owners begin planting early and others do so at the last
minute, we usually have about six odiferous weeks, but I
guess it's worth it to have green lawns all year round. I
often wish, though, that everyone would get together and
decide on a day to plant rye grass, so we'd get it all over
with at once. When my own neighbors fertilize, I avoid
the outdoors or else try to pretend it's springtime—March
with its wonderful perfume of citrus in bloom.

"Let's get inside quickly," Denise said. "Betsy had her
winter lawn put in yesterday."

"Did Michael do the work for her?" I couldn't help
asking.

"With all the money Betsy inherited from her husband?
She has a lawn crew, of course."

"Come on, Denise. You know how commonplace lawn
crews are out here. If they had to depend only on wealthy
people to employ them, they'd starve." Denise, attracted
to Harry Stokes herself, had been convinced that Betsy
married for money. After Harry's death, when I came to
know Betsy, I realized how much she had loved Harry and
was suffering as a young widow, left alone to carry his
child. I'd only partially convinced Denise, for I couldn't
bring myself to tell her how strongly I wished Betsy were
my child instead of the daughter of Michael and his ex-
wife.

As usual, we sat in Denise's cheerful kitchen. "I'll get
paper and pen," she said. "That's the way they always do
it in books."

I took the small telephone notepad Denise handed me
and suggested we use one page for each person, at any
rate those we knew had been with Amy Brookman after
her miscarriage. "I've got Virginia, Faith, Lupe, Jeremy,
Quentin, Leila, Nick, and Tommy," I said. "Can you think
of anyone else?"

"No, but we're sure now that they all had opportunity."

"In the right place at the right time, yes, but that's not the whole story." I drew thick lines under each name while I thought about it. "As far as we've been able to find out, only Faith, Leila, and Nick had access to Coumadin."

"First of all, we can eliminate Leila. I can't believe we have two murderers."

"So we're back to where we started this afternoon— Faith or Nick," I said.

"Let's look at motive next. That should help."

"Now that we've talked to her, do you still believe Faith had a strong enough motive, just to use Amy's death as a deterrent?"

"I can tell from the word 'just' what you think. But Ruthie, the woman seems so nice. Then, all of a sudden, she does something monstrous like taking that poor girl's picture when she was probably completely out of it."

"That's not in the same class as murder."

Denise got up and filled a pitcher with ice cubes. She added iced tea concentrate and water and brought it over to me with a tall plastic glass and a napkin. "I know you drink this stuff all year round."

I thanked her and waited while she reheated some coffee in the microwave for herself. Before she joined me at the table, I pulled out the page with Leila's name. Unfortunately, that loosened the rest of the pages. Why doesn't this ever happen in books, I thought, and then decided I liked loose pages better. This way, we could move them around and try to arrange the various suspects in order of probability.

"Whoever killed Leila must have done it because she found out he or she caused Amy's death," Denise said.

"That seems pretty obvious. But if it was Nick, there may have been a terrible fight after Tommy revealed his affair with Amy."

"Could be. If Nick changed the pills, he probably did it to keep Amy from telling her mother about him in the first place."

"We're back to Faith and Nick again," I said. "I can't figure out a reason for any of the others to want Amy dead.'' I drank some of the iced tea. Maybe the caffeine would help me see what I was missing. The word ''missing'' made me think of Tommy, and I reminded Denise about him.

"If we pinpoint the same person the police are looking for, we may as well leave it in their hands," Denise said.

"This isn't a competition."

She looked embarrassed. "I didn't mean it that way. But, as far as we know, the police seem interested only in Leila's murder. If you're going to clear yourself and prove you didn't make a deadly mistake, we have to discover who switched the pills."

I knew she was right. Although I'd heard from Nick, and no one else, that the family still planned to go ahead with the wrongful death lawsuit, he probably had inside information. Now that Leila was dead, I couldn't see how he would gain from the civil lawsuit, but maybe he was her heir. I'd have to ask Sterling Harraday whether Nick could expect to claim any part of a possible settlement.

We sat in Denise's kitchen for another hour, brainstorming, finding only the most farfetched reasons for any of the others to have killed Amy.

"Maybe her death was an accident," I said.

"Ruthie, you know you wouldn't make a mistake like that."

"I didn't mean that kind of accident. But what if someone wanted to make her condition worse, not expecting the hemorrhage to be fatal?"

"Why?"

I had no answer for Denise. It didn't make sense, except perhaps for Faith Sommers, and I couldn't bring myself to believe that fastidious woman would kill two people to validate her point of view.

Finally, I gathered the pages together, borrowed a paper clip, and placed them carefully into my handbag to study later. I put on the jacket to my jogset and asked Denise to drop me back home.

"Are you in a hurry?" she asked.

"It depends what you have in mind," I said. "But I'm not going back to Faith's place."

"Not there. But could you direct me to Quentin Brookman's? I think we should talk to him."

I considered demurring but then decided we might as well do it. Timidity was not going to clear my name. Besides, I wasn't afraid of Quentin.

In case I couldn't find his condo again, we checked the address in the phone directory and started out to see Amy's father. Unable to think of a stronger excuse, we decided to use the same one we'd given Nick. The more I thought about it, I did want to know whether they still planned to file a wrongful death suit against me.

We arrived at Quentin's condo just before six o'clock that evening, much earlier than on my first visit. Here, there was no fertilizer odor because his complex had desert landscaping, rocks and cactus, rather than green lawns.

In answer to our ring, he pulled aside the drapes and looked out from a front window, motioning to us to wait. We waited a long time for him to open the door, and I wondered what could be keeping him this time.

"Is he hoping we'll just fade away?" Denise whispered.

"If he is, he's very much mistaken."

We were the mistaken ones, however, for Quentin suddenly opened the door and greeted us politely. I introduced Denise, and the three of us stood in the doorway and talked about the weather. This is silly, I thought. I have to get us inside. We need more time to talk about something other than trivialities.

Denise tried to rescue us. "Can we come in?" she asked. "We want to discuss some things with you."

"You can say whatever you have to say right here."

Even Nick had been willing to sit down and talk with us, I thought, but Quentin was acting like a person with something to hide. On the other hand, maybe Nick gave that impression precisely because he was trying to appear innocent.

I decided to begin by telling Quentin how sorry we were to hear of Leila's death, trying not to consider the incongruity of offering condolences first to the live-in lover and then to the husband, not even ex-husband, according to

Jeremy. Although I watched closely, his unyielding expression showed no reaction to my words.

"Thanks," he said and reached behind us to open the door again.

"We're trying to find out who murdered her," I blurted, knowing I had to get his attention before we were ushered out of his condo.

"Look, Jeremy told me you helped get him out of jail, but that doesn't make you a detective."

"I know, but my professional reputation is on the line." He stared at me. "I don't get it."

"If we can all sit down and talk . . ." Denise said.

Quentin's reluctance to invite us in remained obvious, but he must have realized we would not be easy to get rid of. He led the way to his living room, which looked even messier than the time before. All the drapes were tightly drawn, holding in the daytime heat even now that the sun was down and the temperature had dropped. The only light in the room came from a single floor lamp.

I decided to try the positive approach. "Of course, you know now that I had nothing to do with your daughter's death."

"I don't know any such thing."

"The same person who murdered your wife killed Amy," I said bluntly.

He looked like the idea was new to him, but I couldn't judge whether his surprise was genuine or not. "The police never said a word about that." He paused and stooped to make room for us on the sofa by moving some newspapers to the floor. "Neither did Jeremy."

"And that's exactly why we're trying to get information."

Quentin's expression suddenly took on a shrewdness I hadn't noticed in him before. "Sure," he said to me. "You're trying to get off the hook."

"I'm trying to prove what I knew all along—that I had nothing to do with Amy's death."

"Maybe it's the other way around," he said. "Maybe you killed Leila, too."

I could understand Frank Moreway's suspicions of me.

It was his job to suspect everyone, but I wasn't going to take it from Quentin. "Let's be realistic," I said. "Who do you think had a motive?"

"Don't look at me. The police already asked me enough questions."

"Like where you were at the crucial time?"

It didn't work. He simply nodded without revealing what he'd told them. I tried another tack. "We talked to Nick Kenmore this afternoon," I said.

The name caused the explosion I was anticipating. "That miserable creep," he yelled. "Did he confess that he killed them?"

From a purely selfish point of view, I regretted I didn't have a tape recorder with me. It seemed unlikely that Quentin could go through with the lawsuit if I could have recorded that last statement.

"Did you blame Leila for not preventing Nick's pursuit of Amy?" I asked, trying to sound matter-of-fact.

"Of course, I blamed her," he said. "What kind of mother would be so oblivious to what was going on?"

So, he did have a motive after all. Quentin's strong temper was obvious, but would he have admitted his anger so freely if it had led to murder?

He must have understood what I was thinking, for he hurried to add, "But I didn't kill her. And anyhow, I can prove I was at work."

"What do you do, anyhow?" Denise asked. I guessed she was trying to find out if he had the kind of job that Nick did, one he could be away from for a time without causing any particular notice or comment.

"I work in a video store and, for your information, lots of people must have seen me that day."

"Which video store?" Denise asked.

"None of your business. I told that police detective, but I'm not having anyone else hang around asking questions."

I resolved to check it out with Jeremy as soon as possible, but I really couldn't see how we'd discover anything Frank Moreway missed.

"Let's discuss some of the other possibilities," I said.

"You must have your own ideas about who did it."

"Nick," he said flatly.

"He seems to have an alibi."

"I never said Nick was stupid. Naturally, he was sure to think of saving his own skin." Quentin riffled through some of the newspapers he'd piled on the floor. "You're an educated woman," he said, his tone making it sound like an insult. "If you read the papers, you must know how many murderers are never caught."

"That's why we're trying to discover this one. And I'd think you would be at least as interested as we are."

"Just what do you expect me to do, go gunning for him?"

"Of course not. But if you really believe he's the one, you can think back to how he acted the time you were all at Virginia's, the night before your daughter's death."

For the first time, I saw sadness replace the angry expression in his eyes. He looked grim. "How do you know we were all there?"

"You're wasting time," I said, as firmly as I could. "Just try to remember anything you noticed, especially anything out of the ordinary."

He seemed to try, taking on a look of intense concentration, like a child trying to remember where he lost his newest toy. "It's hopeless," he said after a while.

"Where was Amy?"

"Lying down on the living room sofa, covered with some kind of throw thing—an afghan, I guess you call it."

"Did you see any medicine vials?"

He closed his eyes and concentrated again. "I don't know. Maybe. Virginia had set up a tray table with stuff on it for Amy, so she didn't have to get up."

"And was Nick alone with her at all?"

"Not while I was there."

This wasn't doing any good, so I decided to try something else. "What about the boy? Tommy?"

Quentin suddenly seemed uneasy. "Why bring him into it? I thought we agreed it was Nick."

"We can't be sure. You know that," Denise told him. "And Tommy could have been upset enough with Amy to want to punish her by changing the medication. Maybe he didn't expect to cause a life-and-death situation.''

"And you have to admit his disappearance is suspicious,'' I added. ''Even the police are looking for him.''

Quentin was absolutely still except for his eyes, which seemed to dart to the doorway leading to the back of the condo. I had just time to wonder what he was hiding when Tommy walked into the living room, holding a large kitchen knife.

Twenty-two

My first shocked reaction was to blurt out, "You're in it together." Then I tried to hide my fear, knowing Denise and I were no match for the two of them. My forehead glowed with perspiration, but I didn't dare move to pull a tissue from my pocket.

"Aren't you being rather silly?" Quentin asked. "Tommy had nothing to do with the murders. And neither did I," he added almost as an afterthought.

"Then why the knife?" I asked, trying to control the shakiness in my voice. "And why are you hiding Tommy? You know as well as we do that the police want to question him."

"So they can make another mistake like they did with Jeremy? My brother's a big guy. He can handle himself in any situation. But look at Tommy. How long do you think it would be before he'd confess to anything so they'd leave him alone?"

I turned to Tommy. "But why did you run in the first place?"

He was wearing jeans and a clean white T-shirt that must have been Quentin's because it was much too big on him. Rubbing the back of his neck with a nervous gesture, but still holding the knife in one hand, he stood there, not making eye contact with us.

Quentin sighed. "Now that you showed yourself, you might as well tell them everything."

"I was afraid," he said slowly.

"Of the police?" Denise asked.

"No. That came later when he," Tommy pointed at Quentin, "when he told me about Amy's uncle getting arrested."

"Then who are you afraid of?" I asked.

"The one who killed Amy and her mom."

"You know who it was?" I wondered why I was buying into his story and added, "That doesn't explain why you're pointing a weapon at us."

He reached back to the nearest corner of the room and put the knife down on the floor. I heard myself sigh in relief, but the warmth in the room and my own nervousness made me unbearably uncomfortable. I took off my jacket and tried to appear calm in order to gain information from Tommy.

When he turned to face us again, I realized for the first time that he was more nervous than we were. "None of you listened to me when I told you that other time, and now Amy's mom is dead, too."

I remembered how he insisted Nick had killed Amy. But there was no proof, and I didn't see how there could ever be proof. Whoever switched the tablets would have been careful to avoid being seen. And now, with Faith's recollections, we knew they all had opportunity.

"You can't simply accuse him," I said. "Did you see anything out of the ordinary that night at Virginia's house?"

"Why was he even there?"

"Tommy, we talked about this the other day," Quentin said. "He had to go there with Leila or it would have looked strange."

"He could've found an excuse. No, I tell you he needed Amy out of the way so she wouldn't tell her mom about him."

"You didn't answer the question, Tommy," I said. "Did you notice something? Was Nick alone in the room with Amy at all?"

"I never let him out of my sight," the boy said.

"Then you've just given him an alibi."

"He must have changed the pills before."

"When?"

There was no answer. Tommy looked at each of us in turn and then back to the corner where the knife lay. "Are you going to turn me in?"

"No," I said and was surprised to find I meant it. "But tell me, Tommy, were you still watching Leila's house after the night we met you there?" I could only hope that he'd continued his surveillance and could tell us something he'd kept from the police when he decided to hide instead of talking to them.

"I never went back," he said, but he looked away from us, and I was almost sure he was lying.

I turned to Quentin. "Wouldn't it be better for Tommy to turn himself in? If the police find him here, he'll really look guilty."

"And you'll be an accessory," Denise added.

"The boy and I've discussed this over and over. I misjudged him once, and I'm not making the same mistake again."

"Misjudged him?" I asked.

"You know," Tommy said. "The baby."

"He's okay here, and he'll stay until the cops find the real murderer. I know he's innocent."

"The only way you could be sure is if you did it yourself," Denise said.

I glanced nervously at the knife in the corner of the room. Quentin noticed and smiled for the first time. "Don't worry. I'm *not* a mass murderer. And besides . . ."

Whatever he intended to say was cut off by the doorbell. Tommy immediately turned and disappeared toward the back of the condo, while Quentin moved the drapes slightly and peered out. "Jeremy and Lupe," he said and went to let them in.

"Why's it so stifling in here, Quent?" I heard Jeremy say as he walked into the living room.

"You know why I have to keep everything closed up."

"No one's going to look for . . ." Jeremy stopped in midsentence as soon as he saw Denise and me.

So Jeremy knew where the boy was and hadn't told Detective Moreway either. I wondered if we could all be considered accessories to a crime even if Tommy really was innocent.

"It's okay," Quentin said. "They know."

"What's the use of hiding him if you're going to tell everyone?"

"Look, Jeremy, don't pull the big brother act. I know what I'm doing."

"Why do you think we came over? To talk you out of this harebrained stunt you're pulling."

While they argued, Lupe sat down next to Denise and me. She looked much better than she had on Thursday, with more color in her face and a calmer expression in her eyes. "Did you learn anything from Nick?" she asked.

We told her about our talk with him and also our visit to Faith Sommers. By this time, the others were listening to us. Jeremy started pacing the length of the narrow room. "Unfortunately, you've come up empty," he said.

"Have you any ideas?"

"My advice is for Tommy to give himself up. Right now, the police are wasting time looking for him when they could be searching for the real murderer."

Tommy had reappeared, and we all turned toward him. I could see how frightened he was at the idea of turning himself in, but I couldn't interpret whether it came from guilt or innocence.

"How can you say that after what they did to you?" he asked.

"Listen kid," Jeremy said. "I don't know what you expected, but they didn't beat me or torture me or do anything other than question me over and over again. I guess they were trying to trip me up. Maybe get me to change my story."

"But you didn't run away."

"That's why turning yourself in is the best thing to do. Otherwise, when they find you—and you can't hide here indefinitely—it will look far worse."

We all waited for Tommy's response, but he was silent. Finally, he said, "I have to think about it."

"Okay, kid, but don't take long to decide. The more

people who know where you are, the sooner the word will get out.''

I wanted to assure them that we wouldn't say anything but thought better of it. Maybe it would be smarter for Tommy to go to the police. And if he was hiding something, they could discover it more easily than we could. So far today, while we'd picked up bits of information, the solution to the murders was still tantalizingly out of our reach.

"Jeremy," I said, "and Lupe, too. According to Faith Sommers, you were both at Virginia's house at the crucial time."

"Now just wait a minute," Jeremy said.

"I'm not accusing you. But I've been asking everyone who was there to think back, to recall if they saw anything unusual that night."

"That woman was leaving just as we arrived," Lupe said. "Don't you remember, Jeremy?"

"What woman?"

"The one we always see on television talking about pregnant teenagers. She was wearing a cerise silk pantsuit and long pearl earrings."

"You expect me to remember what a stranger was wearing that night. I don't even know what you were wearing."

"That's not the point," I told them. "But what you just said matches Faith Sommers's story, and that *is* important."

Lupe smiled at Jeremy, and he put his arm around her. For a moment, I wondered whether one of them would kill to protect the other. "Who else was there?" I asked.

They had nothing to add to the facts we'd already gathered even though they'd stayed on for some time talking to Virginia and Leila. I was convinced if I could only find the right questions, we'd be able to discover who'd had the opportunity to change Amy's medication.

"What room were you in, and where was Nick while you three women were together?" I asked Lupe.

"I don't know." She turned to her husband, "Was Nick with you?"

"He was with both of us," Tommy said.

It seemed as if he had given an alibi to Jeremy now, too. And since the women were together, no one had opportunity. The more I considered it, however, the more I realized anyone could have managed time alone in the room with Amy without the others thinking anything about it. Aside from Nick, that is, since Tommy had shadowed him. Even Quentin, who'd left early, could have made the substitution, especially since fewer people were around when he was there.

In desperation, I asked, "Can't any of you remember if somebody was alone with Amy, even for a few minutes?"

"Listen Ruthie," Jeremy said. "Consider everything that's happened since that night. We need more time to think about it."

"Just try to visualize where people were."

"Maybe we should get someone to hypnotize all of you," Denise said. "That's supposed to help people recall things they didn't even realize they knew, like after a hit-and-run accident. They can describe what a car looked like and . . ."

"I'd be willing," Lupe said. No one else responded.

It all seemed so futile. We'd talked to most of the people involved, and we had discovered very little. "Right now," I said aloud, "it looks like everyone and no one had opportunity. And let's face it, the two people with the strongest motives were never out of sight of each other."

"Sometimes a negative can be a positive," Denise said.

Before I had a chance to ask what she meant, the doorbell chimed again. "What is this, the state fair?" Quentin said as he pushed the curtains aside again.

"Be firm," Jeremy told him. "Don't let anyone else in."

"I don't have much choice. It's Virginia."

This was a lucky break, I thought. She was the only person we hadn't been able to question about the crucial time period.

Virginia walked into the living room, looked at the littered floor and made a sound that signaled her distaste for the mess. "Aren't you ever going to clean this place up?"

''Some of us aren't so uptight about neatness,'' Quentin answered her.

This was only the third time I'd seen Virginia, but it was obvious she took considerable care with her appearance. Although Denise was well-coordinated in a trendy way, and I always strived to look professional on work days, Virginia's style seemed rather formal for the casual chic that was the norm in Scottsdale. And despite the uncomfortable warmth in the condo, she kept on the jacket to the slate gray suit she was wearing.

She must have a wardrobe of crisp white blouses, I thought, for she was wearing still another one today. At first, she didn't seem to notice Tommy; she was so intent on what she had to say to Quentin.

''I came to tell you I think it's disgraceful you allow that worthless man to live in my sister's house. You own the house now, and it's up to you to get rid of him.''

''Eric tells me I can't just throw him out. There's all kinds of legal stuff involved.''

''Then get another lawyer.''

Jeremy joined the argument. ''We can't change lawyers. You know Eric's a cousin.''

''Much good he did with the other business.''

Both Jeremy and Quentin glanced nervously in my direction, and Virginia followed their gaze. I expected her to comment; in fact, I thought she'd be as vehement as she'd been at the demonstration, but she said nothing. She merely continued to look around the room until she noticed Tommy for the first time.

''Don't say it,'' Quentin told her.

''Maybe you could tell my sister how to think, but no one tells me what to say. Leila would be alive today if she didn't let men run her life.''

''So you also believe Nick killed her,'' I said.

''Or him.'' She pointed to Tommy, but before anyone had a chance to challenge that statement, she turned to Quentin. ''I intend to stay until I get some answers from you. So you may as well find me a chair.''

Jeremy and Tommy were both standing, while Lupe, Denise, and I had the sofa. Quentin, who had returned to his recliner, jumped up and went out of the room, coming back with the rickety folding chair Tommy had used the last time we were at Quentin's condo. He opened it carefully and placed it next to Virginia. She brushed off the seat, making sure we all noticed, and sat down.

I decided I wasn't going to lose the opportunity. "We've been trying to place all the people who were at your house the night before Amy died," I said. "So far, no one seems to have been alone in the room with her long enough to have switched her medication."

"You are still trying to deny your responsibility, I see."

"Let's be realistic, Ms. Rowland," I said. "Your sister's murder changed the scenario."

"And whom do you accuse?" she said, sounding like a long-forgotten high school English teacher of mine.

"I'm not accusing anyone. I just feel if we learn everything possible about that night, it will start to make sense. One thing we need to know is when Amy began taking her medications. She came into my pharmacy so late in the day that . . ."

"You are entitled to do what you want with your time. But I am here to get something settled with my brother-in-law."

"Ex," Quentin said.

"That's exactly the point. You and Leila were never legally divorced, so the house will belong to you."

"Virginia, this isn't the time to discuss the house. We have more important things to consider," Jeremy told her.

"Such as?"

"I agree with Ruthie. We have to reconstruct what happened the night before Amy died." Jeremy stopped for a moment, and I could see he was still having trouble controlling his grief. To me, he seemed of all the family to have taken his niece's death the hardest. Either that, I thought suddenly, or he was reacting to his own guilt.

"Also," he said, "we're trying to get Tommy to turn himself in."

"Let us take the two things in order," Virginia said. "A constant stream of people came to the house that evening. Amy was exhausted, and I made her comfortable on the davenport in my living room." She paused. "All of us were in and out of that room."

"But was anyone alone with her?" Denise asked.

"I cannot be sure. It seemed so obvious to me that the wrong medication came from the pharmacy that I never considered anything else."

"And now?"

"What you say seems logical, unless Leila was killed for an entirely different reason."

"What reason?" Denise persisted.

"My sister did not have much other than her house." She looked at Quentin. "He inherits that and everything in it."

"Maybe she left it to you," Quentin countered.

"I happen to know she did not have a will, so with Amy gone, too, you are the one."

"Are you trying to say I killed two people . . . my wife and daughter . . . for a house." He was so indignant that the words tumbled out. ". . . not even an expensive one . . . and with a mortgage besides."

"You bought that house before Amy was born. I happen to know the mortgage is nearly paid off."

"If that's what you think of me, why did you come in here urging me to take the house over?"

"I wanted to see your reaction," she said calmly.

We'd all seen his reaction, but now I wondered if his supposed lack of interest in the house was a cover-up. And I remembered, too, the night I'd been here with Jeremy, when Quentin had threatened both Leila and Nick.

"Now let us talk about this young man." She turned to face Tommy, who started fidgeting when she looked at him. "If you are innocent, why are you hiding here?"

Quentin began to explain what he'd already told us, but Virginia interrupted him. "He can speak for himself."

"I dunno. I was afraid Nick would kill me, too."

If we stayed here long enough, I thought hearing the slight change in Tommy's story, I'd suspect everyone all over again, but maybe we'd eventually reach the truth.

"Then the safest place for you is in police hands," Virginia said.

Tommy suddenly looked like a boy whose teacher had threatened to keep him after school. "I guess you're right," he said.

Virginia wasn't through organizing everyone. "You had better go with him," she told Quentin. "The rest of you can clear out. And don't think I'm finished with you, Quentin. I will wait right here until you get back."

Twenty-three

Virginia Rowland crossed her arms and sat back on the folding chair as if she were in a comfortable armchair, a pose meant to signal that she really intended to wait him out. The rest of us looked from her to Quentin. He said nothing at first, then sighed, and leaned forward to pick up his keys and a baseball cap from under one of the newspaper stacks.

"Okay, everyone," he said. "I guess we may as well do what the lady says."

I felt dazed as Denise and I walked to the front door. Quentin opened it and stood there while everyone filed out. Once outside, he handed the cap to Tommy.

"Here, put this on, so no one recognizes you before we get to the police."

We watched as Tommy and Quentin got into the latter's pickup truck. Lupe and Jeremy had parked their pickup in the driveway, and they left a minute later.

"Do you think one of them is the killer?" Denise asked as we continued on to her car.

"I'm more confused than ever," I said, "but let's sit in the car and add what we just learned to those pages we filled out at your house."

Denise stopped walking abruptly. "Did we take them with us?"

"Oh, God," I said.

"Well, don't worry. If you left the lists at my house, we can drive over to work on them there."

"That's not it. I left my jacket back there." I nodded in the direction of Quentin's condo. "I really don't want to face that woman again. I'm sure *she* never forgets anything."

"It's no big deal. I'll go with you."

We retraced our steps and pressed the doorbell again. Virginia opened the door in immediate response to the chimes. "Well?" she asked.

"Ruthie needs her jacket."

"And this is the woman who claims she does not make mistakes."

"I don't make professional mistakes," I said.

"I have been straightening up this pigsty," Virginia said. "Not that he will appreciate it."

"Then you found my jacket?"

"I did not get to the living room yet. The kitchen is in worse shape."

She led us out of the dark hallway into the living room, and I saw that she had removed her own jacket and rolled up the sleeves of her blouse to work in the kitchen.

I stared at her arms as she walked ahead of us. They were covered with bruises.

For one wild moment, I thought Nick had assaulted her and then I understood. This was the elusive fact I'd been trying to pin down. If Leila, the younger sister, was taking a preventive regimen of Coumadin because of heart disease in her family . . . My heart beat crazily as I finished the thought. Of course, Virginia would also be on Coumadin.

What would her motive for murder have been, I wondered. Maybe she had to get rid of Leila because Leila knew about the Coumadin, but what possible reason did she have to kill Amy?

Virginia scooped my jacket off the sofa, turned, and handed it to me. I couldn't take my eyes from the black and blue marks on her arms in time. And I saw immediately that she was aware of my discovery. We stared at each other. Then in one swift movement, she reached down and picked up the knife Tommy had dropped.

"So, you are quite the knowledgeable pharmacist after all," she said.

I knew Denise was behind me, out of Virginia's reach. "Run, Denise. Get out of the house and call the police."

"Oh, no you don't," Virginia said. "If one of you tries to leave, the other will be dead before she reaches the front door."

"We'll be dead anyhow. Go on, Denise. Don't listen to her."

Denise didn't move and, in a moment, it was too late. Virginia took a few steps to the side to position herself so she could lunge at either of us, and I knew that even though there were two of us, we were no match for a determined woman with a large knife.

"I want you both to walk very slowly to the sofa and sit down."

We searched each other's faces, looking for a way out but realized we had to follow her instructions for now. My mind was darting frantically over the possibilities. Could we both rush forward simultaneously, one grabbing the knife hand and the other holding on to her? How could we coordinate such a move when she was standing only two feet away and could hear any word that passed between us?

I thought of the Mace canister in my handbag. It had saved me from a determined murderer once before but, although my handbag was still on my shoulder, there was no way I could open it and extract the Mace while Virginia Rowland watched us.

She seemed to be deciding what to do next, and I forced myself to appear calm and make her realize she would be caught if she tried to kill us. No, that wasn't the way to go about it. I had to treat all of this as some inexplicable mistake.

I saw Virginia reach for the folding chair she'd occupied before and use one foot to pull it toward herself. Denise started up.

"Get back there," Virginia shouted at her, waving the knife. Denise obeyed.

Even seated, now only a foot or so in front of us, Virginia looked formidable. "Too bad you were so careless to leave your jacket behind. Or was that just an excuse?"

"I don't know what you're talking about," I said. "It was so warm in here, I forgot all about needing the jacket until I got outside."

She stared at me without speaking, and I tried again. "Look, I know you think I was to blame for Amy's death, but let's allow the courts to settle it. You don't really want to harm the wrong person. Besides, Denise had nothing to do with it one way or the other."

"Good try," she said with what sounded like a choked-off laugh. "I saw your face when you noticed these." She used the point of the knife to indicate some of the larger bruises. "Coumadin side effects. You know all about them, but you never saw me with my arms uncovered until now. No one ever does."

"I don't understand," Denise said.

"She doesn't know what you're talking about, Ms. Rowland," I added. "Let her leave."

"You underestimate my intelligence."

"No, I'm sure you're very bright," I said. "I saw how well you organized everyone tonight."

"That was easy. I wanted to give the police every opportunity to question Tommy. And if they let him go, there is always Quentin and his claim to the house." She was still enunciating each word clearly, although I guessed her stress must be nearly as great as my own. How could she kill two more people and get away with it?

As if she knew exactly what I was thinking, she said, "The hard part is arranging your deaths. But I will figure it out."

"We never even suspected you," Denise said. "Every time your name came up, we didn't have a motive for you."

"So now you want to keep me talking. I told you not to underestimate me."

"I should have known it was you. You're the only one who heard me tell Amy to take the purple pills four times a day to stop the bleeding."

"You are right," she said, as if she were a teacher praising her student for giving the correct answer to a difficult problem. "That is exactly when I realized I could exchange those pills for my blood thinner." She waved her knife hand at me in an admonishing gesture. "It was all your fault. You should not say 'purple' when you mean 'lavender.' "

"Not everyone knows what I mean if I say 'lavender' or 'orchid.' So I just use 'purple' as an all-inclusive color," I said and then realized how ridiculous it was to defend myself this way. Virginia's rational tone was so at odds with the absurdity of the words that I had tried to respond logically.

"Then it is your job to educate them."

"I don't want to argue with you, Ms. Rowland."

"Then, be quiet."

"Sooner or later, the police will figure out you take Coumadin," Denise said.

Virginia made that choked-off substitute for a laugh again. "The police will never even think to check on that. They are not familiar with drugs like your friend here. Legal drugs, that is."

"For your information," Denise told her, "Ruthie's very good friend, who's also a pharmacist, is checking on Coumadin prescriptions. He'll catch on and tell the police."

"Denise," I said, horrified at the idea that Virginia would go after Michael next.

"Don't worry, Ruthie. She doesn't know who he is or where to find him."

I understood what Denise was trying to do, but I could see it wouldn't work. We were an immediate threat, whereas Michael, and she couldn't be sure he really existed, was a farfetched supposition. Since Virginia wanted quiet so she could plan, we had to keep her talking.

"What I can't understand is why you killed Amy. Everyone said she was like a daughter to you."

Her face softened into blurry lines, but the knife never wavered. "That's why," she said. "She killed my grandchild."

I gasped. "But it wasn't her fault; it was a miscarriage."

"That's what Amy said," Virginia shouted. "But I was sure she lied to me. She kept talking about an abortion, and I thought she had one behind my back."

"Weren't you with her when she miscarried?"

"I was at work. Amy called me from the doctor's office, saying she was too weak to cope. She wanted me to come and get her, so I left work and picked her up," Virginia gave me one of her dour looks. "That is when we came to you for the medications."

"By then you must have known what really happened," I insisted.

"I knew only that she killed my grandchild."

"You thought it was Tommy's baby, didn't you?"

"What difference does it make? It was Amy's too. I would have treasured it."

Despite the terror of our situation, I thought of my own mother singing that her jewels were her children, and I pitied Virginia. All three of us were childless, I reminded myself, but that wasn't a license to kill.

"And Leila?" Denise asked.

"When I found out about Nick and Amy, I confronted her. I should have waited until I was calmer to talk to her."

"She guessed?"

"I argued with her. If she had been a good mother, none of this would have happened."

"You can't know that," I said.

"When Amy lived under my roof, I took good care of her."

Until you killed her, I thought, but didn't allow the words to escape. I started thinking again about ways for us to free ourselves. She was only one person and we were two. Surely, even though I knew rage would give her additional strength, we could overpower her. I looked carefully at the knife, trying not to give myself away. It was a heavy-duty meat knife with at least a six-inch blade. If I did try to take it away, she could plunge it into me before I succeeded. I decided to see how she planned to dispose of us first. Maybe if she took us somewhere by car, we could get away more easily. She'd have to let one of us drive and wouldn't dare knife that one or the car would go out of control.

Although I wanted to keep her talking, my throat had dried, and I felt that I couldn't get more words out. I would give her a chance to think, to realize we had to leave the house.

Her eyes moved from Denise to me, but they weren't quite focused. I knew, however, that as soon as one of us made a move, she'd be on us with the knife. When she finally spoke, I nearly gave up hope.

"You two will be victims of a fire," she said. "When I finish burning this place down, no one will know how you died."

I conquered my fear enough to speak. "They can tell," I assured her. "And they'll know you stayed on here."

"Ah, but I will be the only one left to tell what happened. And I can assure you, I will have a solid story ready."

Twenty-four

Her intention to dispose of us right here in Quentin's condo meant I'd have to figure out another escape plan. I stared at Virginia, trying to gauge whether she would kill us first or depend on the fire. The horror of being burned alive engulfed my mind so that I couldn't think of anything else. Then I realized if she were not too far gone, if she had any sense of self-preservation left, she couldn't trust that the fire would burn long enough to be fatal.

"You're crazy." Denise hurled the words at Virginia as if she were firing them from a weapon. I knew it was the wrong thing to say, but there was no way to stop her. Now, I was sure Virginia would lose control and kill us at once.

"Too bad you will not be around to see how far I am from craziness," she said.

It seemed impossible that such a cold, calculating woman could have killed because she wanted to be a surrogate grandmother. I thought of something else to try. "If you let us go, you can say Amy's death was an accident."

"Go ahead, talk," Virginia said. "We have plenty of time. It will take the others hours to make their statements to the police." She now sat so far back on the folding chair, I prayed she would overbalance. "Besides," she continued, "the later it is, the less likely anyone will notice the fire and interfere."

"You had no way of knowing the blood thinner would cause a fatal hemorrhage."

"Well done, madam pharmacist."

I could see she was toying with us now, enjoying her power and not wanting to cut short her triumph over us. "You can still claim it was an accident."

"Perhaps I could. But then again, they will ask why I did not get medical care for Amy before it was too late."

"I'm sure you could come up with a good reason. Maybe you were out of the house when her condition became critical."

"Maybe I was."

I leaned toward her eagerly. "Then let us go. You have a better chance that way."

"But you forget my dear sister."

I hadn't forgotten Leila at all, but I'd hoped she would—at least long enough to let down her guard. "Wasn't that an accident, too?" I asked, trying to sound guileless.

"Hardly."

"But a good lawyer can . . ."

"That is not a risk I care to take," she said with finality.

Think, I told myself. If she's going to start a strong enough blaze, she's got to use something like gasoline or lighter fluid. She won't be able to sit here and hold that knife pointed at us. When her preparations force her to divide her attention, that will be the time to break away.

I realized almost immediately that I was wrong. She would kill us beforehand; she couldn't watch us and start the fire at the same time. We would have to save ourselves very quickly or it would all be over. Only her need to wait for the neighborhood to settle down was keeping us alive.

I glanced sideways at Denise, wondering if she also was trying to devise a way for us to escape. She was pale, but only her eyes, blinking unusually fast, betrayed her nervousness.

"How will you explain the fire?" Denise asked.

"Are you worried for my sake or for your own?"

"Curious."

"I changed my mind, if you must know."

Hope leaped into my heart even though I knew she couldn't let us go. "What did you decide?" I asked.

"Does it really matter to you? You will both be just as dead."

I found I had to clear my throat again before I could speak. "What are you going to do with us?"

"This is an older complex. Lucky for me, unlucky for you—the kitchen is not an all-electric one."

She was playing with us again, still savoring her power. I could picture her at work, running the office with petty restrictions and needless paperwork to control the secretaries. I shivered involuntarily, because I suddenly could see the way her mind was working.

"An explosion," she said.

"What about you?"

"Concerned about me? How touching."

"Curious," Denise said again.

"I will escape miraculously."

Although I knew her plan was absurd, that the police would be able to reconstruct what happened, it was no consolation. She'd be caught, but we'd be dead. Again, I tried to find a way to escape.

I had an idea, but the timing would be critical, and I wasn't sure I could pull it off. After all, I was fifty-five years old, and my reflexes weren't what they used to be. But then again, she wasn't that young either and I was the more desperate of the two of us.

Virginia was still talking, describing how she would kill us first and then take her time setting up the explosion. "Everything is just right for me. The range is gas-powered, and the back door to this condo is in the kitchen. I can let the place fill with gas and toss a match in from the doorway."

"You'll kill yourself, too," I said.

She gave that harsh laugh again. "No need to worry about me. I know how to take care of myself."

She was sitting close, so she could keep both of us in full view. I did notice, though, that she turned her head slightly toward whichever one of us was speaking. The next time Denise talks to her, I told myself, I'll try. We have nothing to lose.

I flexed my right foot carefully and waited, mentally

practicing the maneuver I planned. No one spoke.

Come on, Denise, I prayed silently. Ask her a question. But Denise was quiet. I would have to make it happen. "What do you think, Denise?" I asked. "Will anyone believe in two accidental deaths?"

Virginia was furious. "I do not care what you think," she yelled, leaning forward and waving the knife.

"And what about the police?" Denise asked.

All my senses shouted to do it now, and I threw my jacket at Virginia. At the same time, I quickly stretched my right leg out and hooked it around the bottom rung of the folding chair, forcing it to fall over. I expected the chair to collapse and throw Virginia forward, but I hadn't figured it out right. She and the chair went over backwards.

I didn't wait to hear the knife drop but assumed she still held it. As she fell, I grabbed one of the sofa cushions and threw it over her. She was struggling violently and, for a moment, I was afraid I hadn't succeeded; but Denise followed my lead. We now had two heavy cushions shielding us from the knife. I quickly placed one foot squarely on Virginia's upper right arm, so she couldn't move it. "Call 911," I yelled.

Denise pulled the phone across the room, ready to rush to my side if Virginia tried to dislodge me, but I could tell that the fight had gone out of her. She lay there unmoving, unresisting. I looked down to make sure the fall hadn't killed her.

Only her dark eyes moved. They gazed at me so piteously that I recoiled and nearly walked away. In my entire life, I'd never knowingly inflicted such continuous and deliberate injury on another person. I knew, though, that I had to keep my full hundred and twenty-five pounds on Virginia Rowland's arm until the police arrived. Otherwise, Denise and I would be endangered again. I'd have to come to terms with myself later.

Denise finished the telephone call and stood by my side. "They wanted me to stay on the line," she said, "but I explained that you might need help."

"It will be all right," I said, and I didn't know if I was reassuring myself or Denise.

"Is she dead?"

"No." And to myself, I added, thank God. As the adrenaline rush that I'd needed to overpower Virginia receded, I wanted only to bury my head in the one remaining sofa cushion and cry.

Twenty-five

When the police pulled the two cushions off Virginia Rowland, we could see that the knife point had gone clear through the lower one. She was still holding the knife handle so tightly that they had to pry it away from her, but she offered no other resistance.

We told them our story, and then we drove to the Scottsdale Police Department to tell it again before a police stenographer. Although I'd put the jacket to my jogsuit back on, I couldn't seem to stop shivering.

Detective Moreway arrived just as Denise and I finished signing our statements. He looked grim as he read them over. "We would have gotten to Virginia Rowland sooner or later," he said. But I didn't believe him, especially when he quickly called to someone to release the three people he'd been questioning.

I didn't see Quentin, Jeremy, or Tommy because the police kept us a little longer to go over some of the points in our statements again. I wondered what Quentin would think when he found his condo even messier than he'd left it. Then I realized the condo was now a crime scene, and he'd have to find somewhere else to stay. Maybe he'd room with Nick, I thought and began to laugh.

"She's hysterical," Frank Moreway said.

"No," I told him and quickly fought to control myself.

"It's better than crying," I said to Denise as we were finally allowed to leave and walked to where she'd parked her car.

"As far as I'm concerned, Ruthie, you can laugh or cry or whatever you want to do. You saved my life."

"We did it together," I said. "You were ready when the moment of truth came."

"That's because I trusted you to act in time."

Both of us were quiet, absorbed in our own thoughts, until we pulled into Denise's driveway. This time, because I wasn't expecting Michael at all, I could see him standing on the lawn between the two houses. He seemed to be waiting for us, and I wondered how he knew what had happened.

"Where did you get to, Ruthie?" he asked. "Your car's been parked here for hours, but I haven't been able to track you down."

Then he must have noticed how bedraggled we both looked and started asking more questions. "Are you okay? What's wrong?"

"Come inside," Denise said. "We can talk there."

I saw Michael glance toward his daughter's house, motioning in the direction of Denise's front door. Almost immediately, Patricia came out and joined us. She was wearing beige slacks again with a long-sleeved tailored blouse in beige and black. I looked down at my jogsuit. The pants were grimy, and the jacket had a long tear where the knife must have caught it. I knew most of my makeup had disappeared, and my hair needed to be brushed away from my eyes.

We all followed Denise into her kitchen. "Coffee?" she asked. "Or do you want something stronger?"

"Decaf, please," I told her. The others said they'd had a late dinner and didn't want anything else, thank you.

"Why were you looking for us?" Denise asked as she measured out the coffee into two cups, added bottled water, and put them in her microwave.

"We found another Coumadin patient." Michael seemed rather pleased with himself. "Someone we never thought about."

"Virginia Rowland," I said.

"You knew?" Now he sounded disappointed.

"I know now."

"We should have realized it sooner," Michael said. "Here we are, two pharmacists, and it never occurred to us that if the younger sister was on the drug, it had almost certainly been prescribed for the older sister as well."

"Don't blame yourself, Michael." Patricia placed her hand on his arm. I noticed the colorless polish on her nails and decided to get a manicure first chance I had.

"It looks like you were thinking more clearly than I was, so no harm done," he said.

Denise and I exchanged a rueful look. "Yes, no harm done," I agreed.

"Now tell us what you've both been up to."

We told them. Patricia was the one who turned pale and gasped. "I would have been completely at sea," she said.

"Not at all," I assured her. "You'd be amazed the way danger crystallizes your thinking."

"Or else paralyzes one," she said.

I didn't tell them how I felt when Virginia, literally underfoot, lay there powerless. It would be a long time before I could talk about that to anyone.

Michael said nothing for a while, but a grave expression I remembered from the day we parted thirty-five years ago deepened his blue eyes and showed lines in his face I hadn't noticed before.

The microwave buzzer sounded. Denise took the coffee cups out and handed one to me. I sipped gratefully. No one spoke, and I wondered why Michael was so quiet. I looked up to find him staring at me.

"Sometimes you're very different than the way I remember you," he said finally.

"I guess I am. It was a long time ago."

"Self-sufficient."

"Most women have changed, Michael. We've had to."

"No, that's not it," he said. "You gave me up then because your family insisted on it. Today I think you'd follow your heart."

I looked at Patricia to see her reaction. She sat between Michael and Denise, looking poised and faintly interested in the conversation. Why is he bringing this up now, I asked myself. I had never even told Denise how and why we'd parted.

"Twenty-year-old women were different then. We were girls. But you forget. I was more independent than most, or I couldn't have made it through pharmacy college." Trying to defuse the situation, I looked across the table at Patricia. "Pharmacy schools were just about all male in those days," I explained.

"Yes, Michael told me that."

What else had he told her? I felt betrayed.

Denise looked at my face and changed the subject. "At least, they'll have to drop the lawsuit now."

"That must be a great relief," Patricia said.

I knew I should be overjoyed that I could no longer be accused of a fatal error, and I was thankful. Although my personal life hadn't worked out the way I'd hoped, my professional reputation was now secure. It was time to appreciate what I had and hide my other disappointment.

"Let me thank the two of you," I told Patricia and Michael. "You really did help. I never would have suspected Virginia if you hadn't discovered her sister's medical record."

"Yes, but you would have avoided tonight's close call," Patricia said.

I started to protest that it was better this way, but the doorbell interrupted me. Denise went to answer it and returned with Betsy Stokes. She looked lovely, and I felt a sharp pang because she wasn't my daughter. Her face had rounded with the softened look I often saw in pregnant women. And though I knew that Betsy had been having a difficult time, she seemed serene.

"Hi, everyone," Betsy said and then focused on Patricia.

I watched as Patricia took her hand. "Are you all right, dear?"

"Stop worrying, Mother. I just came over because there's a long distance call for you."

I sat at Denise's kitchen table, trying not to let the others see my stunned expression. It had happened again. I remembered when I first realized Betsy was Michael's daughter. Although I'd never admitted it, even to myself, I had felt overwhelming joy to learn that she wasn't a romantic interest.

This, however, was different. Knowing now that Patricia was Michael's ex-wife offered no relief at all. It was worse to see him involved with her than in a casual relationship. Back with his ex-wife, Betsy's mother, both of them looking forward to their first grandchild—it was too strong a tie to allow any hope for me. And as that realization took hold, I understood myself. Finally, I had to admit how much Michael meant to me.

Betsy remained with us while Patricia left for her call. "It's my stepdad on the phone," she explained to us. "Might as well give them some privacy. That is, if you don't mind my staying here for a while, Denise," she added politely.

We went through the events of the evening all over again for Betsy. By this time I could feel myself starting to fade, and I wanted only to get home and try to get some rest. Despite my better judgment, I had felt a faint glimmer of hope at Betsy's words, but I tamped it down. No way was I going to let myself go through that again.

Betsy was all the audience one could hope for, exclaiming in horror at the appropriate moments. "Dad," she said to Michael. "You're right about Ruthie. She really is someone special." Then she turned to me. "Mother and I think he's like a teenager these days. All he does is talk about you, Ruthie."

RENEE B. HOROWITZ is a professor of technology at Arizona State University. She lives in Scottsdale, Arizona, with her husband and has two sons and a grandaughter. Her authentic, behind-the-scenes look at pharmacy in the Rx series is inspired not only by her pharmacist husband, but also by both their pharmacist dads.

JILL CHURCHILL

"JANE JEFFREY IS IRRESISTIBLE!"
Alfred Hitchcock's Mystery Magazine

Delightful Mysteries Featuring
Suburban Mom Jane Jeffry

GRIME AND PUNISHMENT
76400-8/$5.99 US/$7.99 CAN

A FAREWELL TO YARNS
76399-0/$5.99 US/$7.99 CAN

A QUICHE BEFORE DYING
76932-8/$5.50 US/$7.50 CAN

THE CLASS MENAGERIE
77380-5/$5.99 US/$7.99 CAN

A KNIFE TO REMEMBER
77381-3/$5.99 US/$7.99 CAN

FROM HERE TO PATERNITY
77715-0/$5.99 US/$7.99 CAN

SILENCE OF THE HAMS
77716-9/$5.99 US/$7.99 CAN